The Duke of Nothing

(THE 1797 CLUB BOOK 5)

By

USA Today Bestseller
Jess Michaels

THE DUKE OF NOTHING
The 1797 Club Book 5
www.1797Club.com

Copyright © Jesse Petersen, 2017

ISBN-13: 978-1981546206
ISBN-10: 1981546200

For more information, contact Jess Michaels
www.AuthorJessMichaels.com

To contact the author:
Email: Jess@AuthorJessMichaels.com
Twitter www.twitter.com/JessMichaelsbks
Facebook: www.facebook.com/JessMichaelsBks

Jess Michaels raffles a gift certificate EVERY month to members of her newsletter, so sign up on her website:
http://www.authorjessmichaels.com/

DEDICATION

This is my third anniversary of becoming an indie author.
Thank you so much to the readers, bloggers and friends who
have supported me so much and made this path so successful.

And to Michael, who is the Duke,
no the King,
of Everything to me.

PROLOGUE

1798

Baldwin Undercross watched as his father, the Duke of Sheffield, threw another coin onto the pile before him. The other men in the circle around the table mumbled and grumbled, exchanging looks that spoke of their shock and interest in what was about to happen.

Baldwin felt much the same. It was his first time in a gaming hell and he was not enjoying it, if truth be told. On the top of his mind was how he knew his mother would not approve. After all, Baldwin had just turned fifteen that very day. Without a doubt, she would be horrified and say he was too young.

But his father didn't agree with that assertion. He'd given a very long speech about becoming a man and made Baldwin swear to secrecy where they were going. Still, Baldwin hadn't wanted to come and his father had all but dragged him here.

Despite that, Baldwin had rather liked it…at first. There were beautiful women in abundance, the hell was loud and raucous, and there was much laughter and innuendo in the air. Only, as the hours had progressed, a sense of anxiety had gripped him, increased by the wild and sometimes glassy look in his father's eye as the duke threw more and more blunt in on games of cards, dog fights and now dice. He'd lost more than he won until the last half an hour.

"You certain, Your Grace?" called out one of the men.

"You've already gone double or nothing *and* triple or nothing. Are you sure you wish to bet again?"

Sheffield lifted his gaze and glared at the man. "Mind your business, Carter—no one's asking you. I've got the luck tonight. I should bring my boy more often."

He slung an arm around Baldwin as he spoke, and dragged him into the circle. Baldwin could smell the drink on his father's breath and felt his drunkenness in the way he wobbled on his feet.

"You roll them, boy," his father said, pressing the dice into Baldwin's hand.

Baldwin swallowed hard as he stared at the dice clutched in his trembling fingers. He began to shake them slowly at first, then faster, as he prayed with all his might that he would roll the number his father had placed his bet upon. Eleven. The same age as Baldwin's sister Charlotte.

Eleven, eleven, eleven, he repeated in his mind, as if that would make it happen. He released the dice and they skittered across the table, bouncing in what seemed like slow motion as the room collectively waited to see if quadruple or nothing was a truly good bet.

One of the dice landed first. A six, and Baldwin's heart leapt with pleasure. Halfway there! The second bounced and the sound of it echoed in Baldwin's ears, the only noise he heard even as the men jumped and called out around him. His father's grip tightened on his arm as they watched the numbers skip around. Finally it landed, and all the air went out of Baldwin's lungs.

Four.

The captain of the table chuckled and began to rake in the duke's money as he said, "Tough luck, Sheffield."

Baldwin felt tears stinging his eyes, and he blinked hard to push them back so he wouldn't embarrass himself and his father in front of the room full of sneering men. Slowly he turned and found the duke staring at the money as it was pulled away.

"I'm—I'm sorry, Father," Baldwin whispered, his voice

cracking.

The duke blinked, and it was as if he were being pulled back to the present. He stared at Baldwin with a wrinkled brow and then guided him away from the table and the men and the money he'd lost. "Sorry? Why?"

Baldwin shook his head. "All that money, I-I lost it."

The duke shot him an incredulous look. "Don't be foolish, Baldwin, of course you didn't. It was an unlucky roll, that's all. It's the game, nothing more. But we…we just have to win it back, don't we?"

Baldwin's lips parted. "Win it back? But…but Father, it was so much!"

For a moment, a dark shadow passed over Sheffield's face and he glanced back at the table where the men had gone back to their games, worrying over their own fortunes rather than that of the duke and his son.

"Well, yes," he said softly. "And that's why we can't leave in this state. Come, they're starting a boxing match in the back, and it's a far better bet than dice."

Baldwin's stomach turned. "I-I don't know, Father."

The duke draped his arm over Baldwin's shoulder a second time and gave him a squeeze. "*I* do. After all, wasn't it a thrill when you rolled those dice? Especially when the six came up?"

Baldwin shifted. "I-I suppose so. I thought I might win, after all."

"And you will," the duke reassured him. "You will again. Now I'll show you how to pick a fighter and I'll give you the money to bet. A birthday gift from me to you."

Baldwin hesitated, but finally nodded. How could he not when his father was smiling so brightly and looking at him with such affection? They'd always been close, after all. And his father wouldn't do anything that was wrong. Baldwin knew him too well to believe that. He was just a rich man, with the means to have some fun.

If he said it was all right, Baldwin believed him. So he pushed down the feelings of dread and anxiety, and followed his father through the twisting hallways of the hell. Toward the win his father felt so certain was coming.

The win Baldwin now desired so much that his stomach hurt. The win he wanted more than anything.

CHAPTER ONE

Spring 1811

"Are you paying attention, my love? This is very important."

Baldwin Undercross, Duke of Sheffield, turned from his place at the window and focused his attention on his mother. She was seated on his settee, a slew of papers sprawled out on her lap, on the table before her, on the cushions next to her. She was examining one of them very closely and he barely held back a sigh at her determined expression.

"Yes," he breathed. "So you say."

Her gaze jerked up and held his, the brown eyes so like his own softening a bit. "I'm sorry, darling," she said. "I know you despise this. I would not put you through it at all if it weren't imperative."

He pressed his hands behind his back and clenched them together. The worst part was, she wasn't wrong in her assessment. It didn't make him like what she was doing any more. In fact, he liked it less.

"I recognize that," he conceded with a frown pulling hard on his lips. "After all, if our status is revealed, it could be very…bad. It is what it is. I accept it and my responsibility to remedy the problem."

"At least Charlotte is safe from it," the duchess breathed. "I felt like a weight was lifted from me the moment she and Ewan said their I dos."

That coaxed a very rare smile from Baldwin's lips. His beloved younger sister had married one of his very best friends less than six months ago. A member of his duke club, a bonded set of friends who had come together to help each other with the weight of the responsibility they would one day each bear.

Of course, Baldwin hadn't told any of them his troubles, not even Ewan, Duke of Donburrow and now his brother-in-law as well as in spirit. Nor had he told his sister. Too humiliating.

And what was the point of doing so? Charlotte would only fret, and now she was protected, at least, from the situation of their family.

He could not say the same for himself or for his mother. The worst part was *she* didn't even know how truly bad it all was.

"How could your father leave us in this position?" she said, pressing her hands down on the pile of papers with a crunching of the vellum.

"We've been asking ourselves that for five years," Baldwin said softly. "Father lost all our money, he left us with only the entail and its value is…greatly reduced by his poor decisions. Our position in untenable. I owe it to those who hold our debts and to those who live through the bounty of our title and lands to fix this."

She sighed and picked up one of the papers, smoothing it reflexively as she said, "Well, marry a nice heiress and all will be well."

She said it lightly, and Baldwin forced a flutter of a smile for her, but inside his stomach tied into yet another knot. His mother had convinced herself that the list of heiresses that comprised her copious papers would be their family's saving grace, but Baldwin was less certain. He didn't know if a young woman with a dowry of ten thousand or even thirty thousand would be enough to remedy the situation he now found himself in.

After all, even he didn't know about all the outstanding debts. His father had kept terrible books—purposefully, it seemed, to hide the massive obligations he had incurred. To hide the promises he'd made ten times over for the same rights or horse or piece of unentailed property.

Baldwin had been swimming through it for half a decade. He had only recently become aware of at least five thousand additional pounds worth of debt that he had no idea who owned or how to resolve. That had been the breaking point for him. He had been balancing everything on a knife's edge and now…well, now there was no more balancing. No more triage. This was an emergency.

His mother knew none of it, of course. She was aware of the generalities of their financial state, not the minutia that kept Baldwin staring at the ceiling at night.

"Who do you have to present to me today, Mama?" Baldwin asked, shaking off the dark and dour truth of their situation and focusing on the main opportunity he had to solve it.

She held up her stack of papers with a grim look. "We've talked about half a dozen possibilities already, of course. Here are a few more. Lady Winifred, the Earl of Snodgrass's eldest. She has fifteen thousand and a prize racehorse."

Baldwin flinched. He was finished with racehorses, but he could sell the beast, of course, and bring in a thousand more, perhaps. If only Lady Winifred weren't so very dull.

"Very well," he drawled. "And?"

"I've heard Lady Richards is reentering Society this Season. Now she's a widow, of course, but she was settled very well by both her father and the late viscount."

Baldwin nodded. Indeed, the lady had been. She'd earned her money, as it was widely believed in his circles that she had murdered her poor husband. Of course, it wasn't *fact*, and the ladies did not speak of it, so he wasn't certain they were aware. Still, Baldwin remembered the viscount's hangdog expression every time he was forced to go home to his wife, and shuddered.

"She would not necessarily add her coffers to ours," he suggested. "It isn't the same as a dowry."

"Still, we cannot dismiss twenty thousand out of hand," his

mother said, making a mark on the paper that had Lady Richards' name on it.

"No, we cannot," he agreed. "And who else?"

She sorted into another stack and came up with a single sheet of paper. "Ah, here is one! The American. Her father, Peter Shephard, is some sort of...shipping person out of Boston, I think it is. He has brought his daughter for a Season and they say he's shopping for a title."

"They say, do they?" Baldwin said softly. "Do *they* also have a reason why an American would come here to do his shopping when there is so much tension between his country and ours at present?"

His mother shrugged. "Not really. I've heard whispers he may sympathize a bit more with our side in the current environment."

Baldwin scrunched up his nose. Although he was certainly a good British subject and supported his government in all their endeavors, he didn't like the idea of a traitor. Even one from the other side.

"An American?" he groaned, pacing the room and running a hand through his hair. "Have we really sunk so far?"

She set her papers aside. "I don't know, Baldwin, because I am aware you keep secrets from me. But I think you know the answer, don't you?"

He pursed his lips and refused to answer one way or another.

When he had been silent for too long, she got up. "This man is rumored to have fifty thousand to settle onto his daughter, and he is wild about the idea of marrying into a title. What better title is there than that of Sheffield? You are twenty-seventh in line for the throne. That may not mean anything to you or to your friends, but to this man and his very new money, it means a great deal."

"Fifty thousand," he repeated, the words sounding and tasting very bitter. With fifty thousand he could hold off the creditors and invest...not gamble...*invest*. "All right," he whispered. "All right. I will consider your American."

His mother's face lit up, and she pressed a quick kiss to his cheek. She opened her mouth as if to say something more, but before she could, there was the sound of thundering hooves from the drive. Both turned toward the window to see the Duke of Dunburrow's carriage coming to a stop in the round.

"Oh, Charlotte and Ewan are here!" his mother gasped, clapping her hands together.

"Let's greet them," Baldwin said, motioning to the door. She scurried out and he followed, relieved to leave the talk of blunt and heiresses and everything else behind. It was necessary, he knew that, but that fact made it no less oppressive.

More oppressive, actually.

He stepped onto the stone front steps just as one of his oldest and dearest friends, Ewan, Duke of Dunborrow, stepped down. He turned back and held out a hand for his bride. As Baldwin's sister stepped into view, Baldwin caught his breath. There was no denying the happiness she felt. It was written all over her beautiful face as she leaned up to touch her husband's cheek and whisper something to him.

Ewan had always been a serious person. Baldwin understood why. Hell, he was a serious person, himself. But his new brother-in-law's seriousness had come from something deeper. Born mute, he'd spent a lifetime being treated differently, even horribly. But now he looked…bright as he smiled at whatever his new bride had said. He tucked Charlotte's hand into the crook of his elbow to guide her up the stairs.

"They are a handsome couple," his mother breathed, putting words to Baldwin's own thoughts.

He nodded. "Made all the more handsome by their happiness, I think."

She glanced at him briefly, and he saw a flicker of sadness, of regret pass over her face. He ignored it, ignored the twist in his gut at the sight and the meaning of it. And his family reached the top step at that moment to save him from more of it.

"Mama, Baldwin," Charlotte said as she slipped from

Ewan's touch and embraced first her mother, then her brother. Baldwin's smile became less forced as she pulled away and looked him up and down. "Are you eating?" she asked.

Ewan grinned and pulled her back, signing quickly to her. While he generally communicated via writing, he and Charlotte had created their own hand language as children and that made things easier.

"I am not being too pushy," Charlotte laughed before she stuck her tongue out at her husband. "Tell him I'm not pushy, Baldwin—I must have someone have my side."

"Yes, you are," Baldwin laughed. "But I miss your pushiness. Welcome back to London, come in before the skies open up and let's eat so you stop pestering me about my weight."

She swatted his arm gently and then turned back to her husband. They all entered the house and back into the sitting room where Baldwin had earlier been with his mother. The duchess gathered up her papers as Charlotte poured tea for everyone. Baldwin stood aside as his little family buzzed and interacted. He was happy for Charlotte and Ewan. They had not had an easy time coming to accept their love and their future. But here they were. And in fact, they were the fourth of his large group of friends, his duke club, that had found such powerful and beautiful love in the last year.

And here he was, preparing for a Season where he had to find a wife. Full stop—that was his only job for the next few months. And yet he wasn't looking for love like Charlotte and Ewan had found. He would have no soul mate, no person he looked at like she was the only person in the world. No person who would love him for all his faults and failures, as well as for the title that hung around his neck.

No, he was looking for a mercenary lady who would fill his coffers for the benefit of being called "Her Grace".

He resented that. In that moment, as he watched Ewan rest a hand on Charlotte's lower back while they stood across the room with the Duchess of Sheffield, Baldwin resented it like hell.

But there was no way around it, it seemed. He had not set this ball to rolling down the hill, but he hadn't stopped it, either. He had, in fact, added to its weight after his father's death with his own bad decisions and equally bad impulses. So if he did not get the happy ending of his friends and his sister, perhaps he deserved that.

Ewan met his eyes and tilted his head slightly. He signed something to Charlotte and then began to cross the room. "Bollocks," Baldwin muttered, but he smiled as his brother-in-law came to his side. "Donburrow."

Ewan dug into his pocket and withdrew a silver notebook and short pencil. Swiftly, he wrote a few lines and handed it over. *"What's wrong?"*

Baldwin drew in a long breath. "You know, everyone keeps asking me that. Do I look so very terrible? I'm beginning to feel insulted."

If he had hoped Ewan would smile at his jesting, he was disappointed. Instead, Ewan wrote, *"I'm your friend. Can't you tell me?"*

Baldwin squeezed his eyes shut. How often had he wished to tell his friends about his position? Especially as the dire straights he was in became more and more clear. He knew he would find their support and sympathy if he spilled his secrets.

But he would also find their judgment. For how could they not judge him? He'd made things worse by acting just like his father. He didn't want them to know that while he pretended to be honorable and decent and settled that he was a wastrel.

And beyond that, he also knew that if he whispered to Ewan the truth, Donburrow would immediately offer help—in the form of blunt. So would all of his friends. And that humiliation was perhaps worse than he could bear. To have his friends heap charity upon him, to have them talk about him behind his back in subdued, mournful tones, to owe them more than he did just for their friendship?

No, he had some pride left.

"It's nothing, I assure you," Baldwin said softly, turning his face so that Ewan wouldn't press.

His friend let out a sigh, but if he intended to pry further, he was cut off when Charlotte called out, "Do stop glowering in the corner, you two, and come join us."

Ewan gave Baldwin one last look. One that needed no written translation. A look that told Baldwin that Ewan was there for him. That he would help if it were needed.

Baldwin clapped him on the shoulder. "I know," he said. "Now come on. You should know better than most that my sister will not be denied."

Ewan's face brightened a bit and they walked together to join the ladies for their tea. With great effort Baldwin shook off the resentments, he shook off the weight on his shoulders. The first ball of the Season was in two days. Until then, he was going to enjoy his last few hours of freedom.

Until then, he was going to do his damnedest to forget what the future held. And what he was bound to do in order to save it for them all.

CHAPTER TWO

The Rockford Ball had been the launch of every Season for five years running. Lady Rockford took great pleasure in choosing themes and dressing her poor servants in livery to match them. This year she'd chosen a fairyland as her theme and had draped her ballroom in gauzy blues and greens. Her footmen were styled much the same, and from their frowns and blank expressions, they did not enjoy the small wings that had been affixed to their attire.

Baldwin might have smiled at the silly display, but at present he was surrounded by friends—married friends. The Dukes of Abernathe, Crestwood, Northfield and Donburrow were all waxing poetic about wives and home lives and, in James's case, children.

"How is little Beatrice?" Simon, Duke of Crestwood asked. "I see you finally convinced Emma to leave her alone for a night."

James, Duke of Abernathe, arched a brow. "You saw Bibi yesterday. She is little changed since then. Though she's perfect, so thank you for inquiring. And I can see Emma watching the time even from across the room, but she frets for nothing."

Baldwin followed James's loving stare to find Emma standing with Charlotte, Simon's wife Meg and Graham's wife Adelaide. They were laughing together, fast friends. Would any woman he chose for her purse fit into their set? And if she didn't, would he slowly be eased out of their circle?

"What are you frowning about?" Graham, Duke of Northfield, asked as he jostled Baldwin's shoulder gently.

Baldwin scowled playfully. "I just don't understand how I came to be sucked into the circle of old married dukes. I'm still free."

The others chuckled, but Baldwin saw Simon and James exchange a brief look. His chest tightened at the sight of it.

"There is a rumor, you know, that you are intent on finding a match this Season," Simon said.

Baldwin arched a brow. "And who started this dastardly rumor?"

The group turned toward Ewan en masse, and he shrugged and raised his hand without so much as a sheepish expression.

Baldwin folded his arms. "Let me guess. My mother told my sister, who told you, and you told Simon, who told everyone because he has a big mouth?"

Simon glared, and Graham laughed, "That is essentially the line of progression, yes."

Baldwin rolled his eyes and fought desperately not to have the truth of his situation revealed by his reaction. "Well, there is no use trying to hide it. It's true. I do intend on finding a wife this Season. It's time."

Graham pressed his lips together. "Time really has nothing to do with it. Marry when it's right, not when it's time."

Ewan nodded enthusiastically as James said, "Truly, Graham is right. Marry for love, Baldwin. You deserve all the happiness your friends have found and even more."

Baldwin shoved his suddenly sweaty hands behind his back and forced a smile. They meant well, after all. They didn't know the truth.

"Well, I'll certainly take your advice into consideration," he said. "You know everyone is in town at present. Well, everyone but Lucas. We should get together if you can separate yourselves from your wives."

The men exchange a look and then James nodded. "Capital idea. I'll make the arrangements and send an invitation when we have the particulars managed."

Baldwin exhaled in relief, for his suggestion had taken some of the focus off his very foggy future. "And now I'm going to take some air before I throw myself into this endeavor. Good evening. I'm sure I'll speak to you all later in the night."

They said their goodbyes and Baldwin left then, feeling four sets of concerned eyes on him with every step he took away from them. He exited as swiftly as he could, heading out onto the terrace where a cool late spring breeze hit him in the face and cooled his now-heated cheeks.

Lord and Lady Rockford were possessed of a large veranda, one that stretched the length of their massive home. There were couples and small groups scattered just outside the ballroom, enjoying the air. Baldwin flinched. The last thing he wanted in this moment was to get caught up in meaningless conversation. There would be plenty of that in the weeks to come.

He smiled at those around him and moved away, down the veranda, past the doors to other parlors and into a slightly dimmer corner. He was about to settle in to a perfectly dark and cozy brood when a young lady stepped out of the shadows and placed herself at the wall with her back to him.

She was slender, with a mob of auburn hair piled high on her head in a mock-Grecian style. Tendrils curled from the mass, making little trails across her shoulders that disappeared from view when she adjusted her shawl a bit higher.

She had not noticed him as of yet, it seemed, for her attention was lifted. She was raptly focused on the sky above, and he followed her gaze and caught his breath. There was no moon and the sky was lit up with stars. He took a silent step closer and thought he heard her whispering beneath her breath, though he couldn't make out what she was saying.

He wrinkled his brow. He had no idea what this young lady was doing, but it was evident she did not wish to be interrupted. He was about to turn and step away from her when she stopped murmuring, stiffened and then pivoted to face him.

His heart stopped beating. She was…stunning. It was the

only way to describe her. With fine, delicate features and pale green eyes the color of spring leaves. Her red hair framed porcelain skin, disrupted only by a fetching blush that now colored the apples of her cheeks.

"Hello," she said.

His eyes widened further at her accent. American. This was *the* American.

"H-hello," he repeated, taking a step toward her. "I didn't mean to disturb you."

She smiled, and her pretty face transformed into something exquisitely beautiful. It was a rather crooked smile, with something wicked to it. She looked like she liked to laugh, and it made him want to do the same.

"You didn't," she reassured him. "I just felt silly being caught at…well, being caught."

He wrinkled his brow. "Yes, you were looking at the stars. But I thought I heard you talking."

The blush on those cheeks darkened a shade, and she darted her gaze away as she worried her hands against the stone veranda wall. "Oh, gracious, I must seem like such a ninny to you."

He tilted his head. "Far from it. But I am curious. Were you casting a spell or wishing on a star?"

She laughed and the sound echoed in the air like music. He found himself smiling immediately, and it wasn't one of the forced or pretended smiles that he'd been displaying as of late. It was a simple reaction to her complicated lightness. Like she was a beacon in his darkness that he could follow.

He blinked. Was he waxing poetic? In his head? About a stranger? An American stranger, at that. The world was truly coming to an end.

"Neither of those things," she said. "I was counting the stars."

He blinked and slowly looked up at the thousands of blinking lights above, then back to her face. "Counting the stars?"

She nodded, as if this were a normal thing to do. All the

rage, even. "I was."

"That sounds like an endless endeavor," he said.

She shrugged one slender shoulder and her wrap dipped a bit, revealing a bit of flesh exposed by her pretty gown. He caught his breath at the sight. That sweet spot between her neck and shoulder looked utterly…kissable.

"Endless does not equate purposeless or pointless," she said, dragging him away from his inappropriate thoughts. "After all, how often are you forced to do something you do not like over and over? When I count stars, it is always a joy. It reminds me there are many things bigger than myself or my silly problems."

He pondered those words. "You are correct, of course. Much of our lives is spent in repetitive nonsense. Counting stars is as good a hobby as endless stitching, I suppose. Or playing or walking round and round in circles in a parlor."

She smiled again. "Well, I happen to like all those silly things, as well."

"An accomplished lady is never silly," he said.

"What about an accomplished gentleman?" she retorted.

"I know hardly any of those," he said, and found himself laughing when she began to do the same. His laughter felt rusty, ill-used lately except when it was pretended.

"I doubt that," she said. "You look like a young man who knows a thing or two. But may I ask why you are skulking about on a veranda while there is a party going on inside?"

"Was I skulking?" he asked.

She shrugged again. "A little."

He sighed and turned his attention back to the brighter part of the terrace and the ballroom that lit it. "Perhaps I skulked a little. It was too hot inside and too…immediate."

He drew back at the words that came from his own lips. He had not meant to say them. Hell, he had hardly ever allowed himself to think them.

"Too immediate," she repeated softly, and the smile faded from her lips. "I think I understand what you mean. Expectation hangs in the air."

He nodded. "It does."

They stood silently for a beat, she staring up at him, he unable to take his eyes from her. It was strange, because the silence felt both charged with heat but somehow comfortable, as if she expected no empty chatter.

He shook his head, trying to clear it of the odd thoughts. "Well, er, that very expectation dictates that I return to the ball. And that will leave you to return to your counting, though I must imagine you've lost your place thanks to me."

She laughed again, music in the wind and pointed upward. "Not at all. I left off right there."

He chuckled. "Very good. Perhaps I will see you inside then."

She nodded. "Good evening."

He inclined his head and slowly turned to make his way back to the terrace doors that led into the ballroom. It was only as he reached them that he realized he had never gotten the young woman's name. Not that it really mattered. He knew who she was.

And after talking to her, suddenly the future felt a little less awful.

Helena Monroe watched as the gentleman entered the ballroom and shut the door behind him. It was only when he had left the terrace that she rediscovered the ability to draw a full breath. She spun back toward the veranda wall, gripping it tightly as she thought of the intruder.

By God, but he was well favored. He was the kind of man whose age was hard to determine, thanks to the seriousness with which he held himself, but she doubted he was above thirty years. He had thick brown hair, the kind a woman wanted to run her fingers through, and soulful, almost sorrowful brown eyes.

When she had first looked at him, he had been very somber, but the moment she coaxed a laugh from him, he had changed.

She had been in England for several weeks and had the opportunity to meet a handful of men. None had been at all interesting to her. Not that it mattered, of course, but still. When a man swept in like the one on the terrace had and took one's breath away…

Well, that was a momentous occasion. She found herself wondering who he was. She supposed she could find out easily enough if she asked after—

She lifted her hands to her mouth. She had never asked his name or given him her own. "He must think you an idiot," she said as she shook her head and looked down over the garden. "And you probably talked too much."

"As you are wont to do, Helena!"

She flinched at the sharp tone of her uncle's voice behind her. She turned toward him, putting as good a face on as she could muster when he was standing there, arms folded, glaring at her. It seemed the only expression he could manage lately.

"Hello, Uncle Peter," she said softly. "I was just getting some air."

He snorted out a nasty sound and arched a brow. "Well, you've had enough air. Go inside. You are here for your cousin, not to indulge yourself in your own foolishness. A lady's companion must stay with her charge."

Helena dipped her head. It was very difficult for her not to retort in the face of such sullen cruelty, but she knew what would happen if she did. Since she had been conscripted into the duty of companion to her cousin Charity, she had felt the back of her uncle's hand more than once.

So she swallowed back her saucy retort and nodded. "Of course, Uncle. I shall go back in at once."

He pointed toward the ballroom doors, as if she would not be able to find them on her own, and waited as she marched her way back to them. Back to the room that was too hot and too loud. Back to the cousin who treated her like a servant. Back to reality that she had escaped for just a moment with a sky full of stars and a handsome man who caught her counting them.

Baldwin stood on the edge of the dancefloor, watching sets of friends and acquaintances spin by in each other's arms. Coming here, he had been expecting to be rubbed the wrong way by such things, but now…

Well, now he had far more pleasant things on his mind than the discomfort caused by the sight of true love. His thoughts kept returning to the auburn-haired beauty on the terrace and the brief connection he'd felt to her.

He was so lost in those thoughts that he did not notice his mother's approach until the duchess touched his arm. "Mama," he said with a nod. "I did not see you."

"No." She smiled. "You seemed leagues away. Are you having a very terrible time?"

He squeezed her hand at the concern in her voice. Whether she pushed him or not, he knew she wanted what was best for him, as much as for the title. If he found love with someone who could also raise their fortunes, she would be over the moon. Which was why he smiled when he said, "You know, I met your American."

Her eyes went wide. "Did you?"

"I liked her," he admitted with an arch of his brow.

His mother's face lit up briefly before a shadow of doubt crossed it. "I am…I am happy to hear it."

"Then why do you look confused?" he asked.

She shook her head. "Well, I only wonder how you managed to meet her."

He blinked at the unexpected question. "How? What do you mean how? How does anyone meet at these crushes? I went out on the terrace to get some air and bumped into her there. We were not formally introduced, but she was…charming."

He had expected his mother's expression to brighten further, but she remained puzzled. "That isn't possible, dear."

"I assure you, it is," he said, and felt the beginnings of irritation. Why in the world did she continue to insist that what he said was not true?

"But Miss Shephard has been dancing for the last thirty minutes, Baldwin," she said, inclining her head toward the dancefloor. "Since before you exited for the terrace."

He followed her gaze to find a blonde woman bobbing around the dancefloor. She was in what looked to be a very expensive gown that matched her blue eyes exactly and was talking—by the looks of it, rather loudly—with her partner.

Baldwin wrinkled his brow. "Who?" he asked.

His mother motioned her head more forcefully. "The one in blue, Baldwin. That is Charity Shephard. Her father is Peter Shephard. *She* is the American heiress."

As Baldwin stared in disbelief at the lady in question, he noticed the terrace door far in the back of the room opened. The woman he had spoken to on the terrace slipped inside, took a deep breath and looked around the room.

"Then who is the redhead by the terrace doors?" he asked.

His mother lifted on her tiptoes and examined the lady. "I'm not sure, but if she was American, I would wager a guess that she is Miss Helena Monroe. That is, Miss Shepherd's cousin, who is acting as her lady's companion during her Season." She clasped her hands together. "Her situation is…not good, I hear. There is some hint of scandal and no dowry to be had."

All the good feelings Baldwin had been experiencing since he found the woman—Helena, he now knew—on the terrace faded away to nothing. Not to nothing. They faded away and were replaced by something different. A horrible, pulsing disappointment. One he ought not feel after meeting the young woman all but once.

"I see," he said.

His mother bit her lip. "You liked the companion?"

He shrugged, dismissing what he felt with less ease than he

should have. "I talked to her for only a few moments."

The duchess bent her head. "I'm sorry, Baldwin."

He patted her hand once more. "There is no need to be. This was never a heart endeavor anyway, was it? It is what it is."

His mother seemed to accept that, although he still felt the trouble in her voice as she changed the subject to other ladies on his list of potential duchesses. He tried to attend to her chatter, but found his gaze returning, again and again, to Miss Monroe.

And the disappointment that had gripped him didn't fade, even though he wanted it to. Even though it had to, and soon.

CHAPTER THREE

Helena carefully unfastened the ivory buttons that lined the back of Charity's very expensive gown and then pushed it forward. Her cousin all but tore it away, tossing it aside on the floor. With a sigh, Helena gathered it up, folding it carefully so Charity's maid, Perdy, could retrieve it for the laundry.

"…everyone watching me," Charity chattered. "I mean, the jealous looks from all the other women, Helena. You wouldn't understand, of course, but it's quite trying to know that all the men want you and all the women hate you for it."

Helena smiled tightly at her cousin and said, "Quite trying, I'm sure. You certainly danced a lot. Were there any men you particularly liked?"

Charity shrugged. "They're all alike, aren't they? Rich, boring as plain toast."

Helena held her tongue. She had no intention of talking to her cousin about the man she'd met on the terrace, not boring as toast at all. Quite the opposite.

"There were no dukes who filled my card, at any rate," Charity continued. "And Papa is really set on that. He says I must try to land one of those before anyone else does this Season. But *you* were the only one close to a duke."

Helena blinked. "A duke? Who?"

"The Duke of Sheffield, of course. You were on the terrace with the man—did you not see him? He's tall, handsome, brown hair, brown eyes. Stern expression. He came back in to the party just as Papa went out to fetch you. You must have seen him."

Helena's lips parted. Charity was describing a man who sounded much like her charming stranger. "I may have seen someone like that, yes."

Charity nodded. "Well, he is looking for a bride, it seems. An heiress, if Papa's sources are right. He's on my list of men to pursue. Did you talk to him? What did you think of him?"

Helena bent her head. So, he was a duke. An heiress-hunting one. That left her out of the equation. She was no heiress. She was a lady with a questionable past who was hardly better than a servant.

"I was outside taking air," she said with a shrug. "I'm afraid your duke…well, he didn't catch my eye."

Charity pursed her lips. "Just like you to miss the most important man in the room. Lordy, Helena, you're meant to be here to help me. If you aren't going to do that, I don't even know why we brought you." She flounced away and took a seat at her dressing table.

"I'm sorry, Charity," Helena said. She wasn't really sorry, but she'd learned quickly that saying it was the best way to soothe her cousin's spoiled side and avoid an argument.

"Well, it doesn't matter, I suppose," Charity said, and the edge was gone from her voice. "Now come and brush my hair."

Helena stood in her place for a moment. "Charity, could you not call Perdy for that? She's going to help you into your night rail anyway, and I'm very tired, myself."

Charity turned in her seat and speared her with a pointed glare. "Perdy isn't any fun to talk to and you were there tonight, so you know what I'm referring to. Anyway, you are my companion, Helena. You're supposed to do as I say, aren't you?"

Helena took a deep breath. Despite her upbringing, or perhaps because of it, she had always tried to find the light in every situation. This one had so little, and her cheeks burned with humiliation as she crossed the room, took the brush from Charity's table and began to stroke it through her cousin's hair.

As she did so, Charity went back to prattling on about the ball. Helena blocked it out as best she could, losing herself in the rhythmic stroke of the brush in her hand. And trying to forget the twinge of disappointment that the handsome man who had brightened her night was one who was clearly out of her reach.

For a woman like her would never catch the eye of a duke. And that was a fact she simply had to accept.

"Are you ready for the tea, dear?"

Baldwin looked up from the latest troubling letter from his solicitor and found his mother standing in the doorway to his study. He blinked and recalled, at last, what she was talking about.

"Er, yes," he said, folding the paper and returning it to its envelope. He glanced at his pocket watch. "When do we begin again?"

She pursed her lips. "In twenty minutes. And some of the more eager mamas may arrive even earlier. I just checked and Walker has the terrace done up beautifully. The weather is perfect and everything is in place."

Baldwin stood and stretched his back as he searched for a smile he could force. "Thank you, Mama, for coming today and making sure all the arrangements have gone smoothly."

She nodded. "Well, I have hopes that soon you will have a duchess of your own who will help you with these things," she mused. "And I will happily retire into role of dowager."

Baldwin stifled a sigh. "Certainly, I will do my best."

She stepped in closer. "I-I know you will, dear. But I hope you'll try to find some enthusiasm for the endeavor. I haven't picked such ogres for you to consider, have I? Some of them are quite pretty. The American, for example."

Baldwin froze. His mother meant the heiress, Charity. No one could deny she was, indeed, beautiful, but when the duchess said *the American*, he could only think of her flame-haired cousin. The witty one, the lovely one, the one who effortlessly made him smile in a genuine way that felt foreign. Helena.

"Yes," he choked out. "The young lady is very fair."

"Very fair," his mother repeated. "Please do wax poetic."

He shrugged. "I promise you, I shall do my best with all your prospects, Mama. I accept the path I am set upon. I have no intention of shirking."

His mother's brow knitted and it was clear she wished to address the subject more, but before she could, his butler, Walker, stepped into the hall behind her. "Pardon me, Your Graces, but your first guests have arrived."

Baldwin nodded. "Ewan and Charlotte?" he inquired.

"No, sir. It is the Duke of Kingsacre and the Earl of Idlewood. I've shown them to the veranda."

Baldwin sucked in a breath. "Kit and his father?"

The earl, Christopher, who everyone called Kit, had been one of Baldwin's friends since they were boys. He was a member of the duke club, though he was the only one who had not yet inherited his ultimate title. Not that anyone mourned that fact. The current Duke of Kingsacre was a wonderful man.

"We'll go to greet them, Walker," Baldwin's mother said with a smile. "Show the rest out as they come, will you?"

The butler bowed away and Baldwin sighed heavily. "Kingsacre's health is declining. Kit has him in town to see a new round of doctors. I'm glad they could both come."

She nodded. "Matthew's mother and I were just discussing it. It is very sad to see such a vibrant man begin to fail. Come, let us go greet them before the rest arrive."

They walked to the veranda together, and as they exited the house, Baldwin was shocked. Kit and his father stood at the wall together, but he would not have recognized the duke had he not known it was him. The once strapping, handsome man was now thin as a reed, he held a cane that he leaned heavily upon and his skin was sallow.

"Kit, Your Grace," Baldwin managed to choke out. "So

glad you could join us."

The two men turned and began to call out their greetings. It was all friendly enough, but Baldwin recognized the strain in Kit's eyes. He loved his father deeply, this slow loss of him was taking its toll, that was clear. Baldwin squeezed his hand a bit more firmly as they shook, and Kit gave him a look of appreciation.

"So fine to be in your home again," Kingsacre said. "I always said you had the best garden in Town."

Baldwin's mother blushed to the roots of her hair and he couldn't help but smile. She had always been very proud of their London garden and continued to oversee its tending even though she no longer lived in the ducal home in Town. At least for the time being. As things got worse, it was possible they'd have to sell her small townhouse.

Kit tilted his head as he looked at Baldwin, then shot his father a look. "Your Grace, would you mind helping me identify what that wonderful-smelling vine is over your trellis just there?" He held out an elbow to the duchess as he spoke.

She nodded and the two walked off, leaving Baldwin with the Duke of Kingsacre.

"Not very subtle, my Kit," the duke laughed.

"I assume that means you wished to talk with me alone?" Baldwin replied, motioning to two chairs beside the wall overlooking the garden.

They sat, and Kingsacre took a deep breath before he spoke again. "My son is worried about you. He says you won't talk to him, but I hoped you might talk to me."

Baldwin shifted and shot a glance toward Kit. "He is wrong to be worried. I could not be more fine."

Kingsacre arched a brow, and even in his fragile state, he did not look like a man one should lie to. Still, his voice was gentle as he said, "I used to see your father, you know. In the hells."

Baldwin broke their stare, looking instead at the greenery below. "Well, many a man likes to game."

"Is that all it was?" Kingsacre asked.

Baldwin swallowed. Once again, he wished he could just spill out the humiliating truth to someone, *anyone*, and have some support. But there was his pride, reminding him that it wasn't only his father's sins he would spill, but his own. He'd always liked this man—he didn't want to be seen differently by him. Nor to have his tale spread amongst all his friends and become a charity case.

"It is nice to see you back in Town," he said, glancing back to the duke with a meaningful look. "Will you stay the whole Season?"

Kingsacre nodded slowly, as if he understood. Then he said, "I shall try, for I believe it will be my last."

Baldwin jolted. "Don't say that."

Kingsacre's expression softened. "I'm an old man, my boy. And a sick one. I have no illusions of where my path is taking me. My son and his friends may not wish to face it, but I am ready to."

Baldwin's throat suddenly felt thick. He knew what it was to lose a father. To many of his friends, this man was as close as they had. To Kit, all that he had.

"And what of your daughter?" he asked softly.

Now Kingsacre's face turned sad. "Juliet is just four. She has no understanding of what is coming. But her brother will care for her well, I know. She will want for nothing."

"Is she in Town, as well?" Baldwin asked.

"I keep her as close as I can these days. When one has love, one should appreciate every moment of it."

Baldwin shifted. Love. That seemed to be a topic in the air as of late. His friends were finding it, encouraging him to look for it. And here he was, on the outside looking in.

"Baldwin," Kingsacre began, but before he could say more, the doors to the house opened and Walker appeared with several of their guests in tow.

Baldwin rose. "I must see to my guests, it seems."

Kingsacre nodded, but his gaze held firmly on Baldwin's.

"You must, I know. But I hope we will talk again soon."

Baldwin executed a swift bow before he turned back to fetch his mother and greet their guests. But as he walked away he felt an increasing sense of ill ease. A feeling he would have to extinguish if he intended on fulfilling the duty that was the only path left for him.

The carriage was too small. Actually, that wasn't true. The carriage was massive, a display of ostentatious wealth that made color flood Helena's cheeks whenever Uncle Peter bragged about it to appalled lords and ladies. But today, with her uncle and cousin sitting across from her, going over their plans and goals, it felt utterly close and hot and uncomfortable.

"Twenty-seventh in line for the crown," Charity said, clasping her hands. "Just think, Helena, you could lady's maid to the Queen someday."

Helena shook off her thoughts and looked at her cousin. "If the King and twenty-six other people happen to all die at once."

"It *could* happen," Charity said with a glare at Helena's comment. "What has you so cross anyway?"

"I'm *not* cross," Helena said.

And it was true. She wasn't cross. She was something else entirely. *Nervous* was probably the best description. She was going to the home of the Duke of Sheffield. The man she knew with almost complete certainty was the same one who had talked with her on the terrace.

The idea of seeing him again, well, it was both exciting and disappointing. She was so far beneath him. It would be obvious the moment he saw that she served her cousin. And yet, she would get to gaze upon that handsome face again. Maybe see one of those smiles that lit up the world.

"Are you woolgathering?" her uncle snapped.

She blinked and forced herself back to reality. "Yes. No.

No."

He glared. "Your duty is to remain close to your cousin, Helena. If there is any chance for her to get near this man or anyone else who is important, she'll need a chaperone so she doesn't look like a wanton. So you go with her."

Helena swallowed hard before she nodded. "Of course."

"Otherwise, stay out of the way as much as possible," he continued. "And Charity, this man could be very important to your future. You could be a duchess or, as you said, even a queen. Wouldn't that be a feather in the family cap?"

"What do you know of the man's circumstances?" Charity asked.

He smiled. "Aside from his lofty title, he has four estates under his protection. Hundreds of workers. He must be worth a fortune."

The carriage turned, and Charity pulled the curtain back to see where they were arriving. Helena peeked over her shoulder, and both women caught their breath at once.

"Oh, he *must* to have a house like this one!" Charity said with a laugh of delight.

Helena tended to agree. The estate was large and beautiful, with an exquisite view of the park across the way. There was no doubt this was the home of a very important and wealthy man. And once again, she was very aware of the disparity of their positions.

The carriage stopped, and her uncle and cousin stepped out. They left her behind to hustle after them up the stairs of the fine house. She flinched at the sharpness with which her uncle spoke to the duke's butler, and then trailed through the hallways toward the veranda, where tea was being held.

Helena couldn't help but look around her as they walked. The house was just as fine inside as out. The furniture was understated and beautiful, the walls done in muted colors. A few portraits graced those walls, and she gasped when she passed by one of the duke standing by a mantel, two large dogs at his side.

It was most definitely the man she had encountered on the

terrace. *Baldwin Undercross, 15th Duke of Sheffield*, the little plaque read.

"Catch up, girl!" her uncle called as they entered a parlor. She scurried to do so, even as her mind spun. *Baldwin.* The name fit him. It wasn't at all common. Nor was he. Of course, she would never call him by that given name. Heavens, she likely wouldn't talk to him at all. The moment on the terrace was one that never should have happened in the first place. Certainly he wasn't thinking about it. She should forget it, too.

The butler opened the veranda door and stepped out. He announced her uncle's and cousin's names to the gathered crowd. "Mr. Peter Shephard and Miss Charity Shephard."

Helena pressed her lips together as they stepped out, Charity looking over the crowd like she was already the queen she imagined she could be by marrying the poor man in that portrait.

The very idea made Helena's stomach turn. She ignored it, shoved it aside and followed them onto the terrace—where she came face-to-face, once again, with the Duke of Sheffield.

To her surprise, he was not looking at Charity or her uncle as he crossed the veranda toward them, an older lady at his side.

He was looking at her.

CHAPTER FOUR

Baldwin's mother was chatting with Mr. Shephard and his daughter, but he hardly heard whatever pleasantries were being exchanged. He was too busy looking at Helena Monroe.

She was even lovelier in sunlight than she had been by starlight. She had a slender, expressive face. Right now the expression was of discomfort, though. When she'd first come onto the veranda, she had met his stare, he had felt the connection he'd felt the first time they met.

But now she was looking at her feet instead of his face. And he didn't like it.

"Baldwin," his mother said, rather sharply.

He jerked his attention back to her and to their guests. "Terribly sorry. Welcome, welcome. I hear you are in shipping, Mr. Shephard?"

Shephard's lips thinned slightly. "Yes, as I just told your mother, my holdings in Boston are vast, indeed. And my father fought on the *right* side of the war forty years ago: yours."

Baldwin wrinkled his brow, uncertain if that was supposed to impress him. He happened to agree that the English side had been correct, but the idea that an American would turn his back on his own burgeoning country still sat badly.

"Very good," he said with an arched brow. "Well, please come and enjoy yourselves. I'm sure we'll find much to talk about today."

His mother shot him a look, then said, "Yes, let me take you to your places."

Mr. Shephard and his daughter followed her away, and Helena moved to go with them, but Baldwin stepped into her path. He hadn't planned to do it, it just happened.

Slowly, she lifted her gaze to his and he forced a smile. "We meet again, Miss Monroe."

"Indeed we do, Your Grace," she said.

"Did you manage to count all your stars?" he asked.

Color flooded her cheeks, but she smiled regardless. That smile. God, but it was fetching. Filled with light and effortless pleasure and kindness.

"Not quite. I've a few more for the next time I'm on a terrace. You are welcome to join me if you'd like."

The moment her words escaped her lips, his mind spun an image of doing just that. Standing on a terrace, *his* terrace, with this young woman. Counting stars with her like he had no care in the world. And then doing more than counting. More than kissing those soft-looking lips. More than a gentleman should do.

He caught his breath as his thoughts went wild and drew back a step. "Well, I should see to the rest of my guests. Your uncle and cousin are just there."

He motioned his hand and then bowed slightly before he strode away. But not before he saw a flicker of hurt and embarrassment cross that lovely face. How he wanted to repair the damage he'd done, but he couldn't.

Just as he couldn't *like* Helena Monroe or allow this strange, immediate and very physical draw to her to develop further. That was an impossibility that he had to put away.

Helena kept a tight smile on her face and nodded along with the conversation at her table. Normally that would not have been a chore. She was seated with her uncle and cousin, yes, but somehow they had also been placed with the lovely Duchess of Donburrow—Baldwin's sister—and her husband, the silent but devastatingly handsome duke. Alongside them were the Duke and Duchess of Crestwood, who were charming companions, as well.

And yet, despite the good conversation and smooth handling of her lout of an uncle, Helena could not be at ease. She kept reliving her encounter with Baldwin...damn it, *Sheffield*...just after she'd arrived.

It was humiliating to think of how he'd approached her and then dismissed her when she'd been so forward. How his face had fallen and he'd all but run away from her. She'd been imagining the man had liked her, just a little, when they talked about stars a few nights before.

Now she wasn't certain he even tolerated her.

"Miss Monroe, you are Miss Shephard's cousin, are you not?" the Duchess of Donburrow asked as she refreshed her tea.

Helena swallowed hard and ignored the pointed look of her uncle. If he had his way she would not be asked anything. He didn't want her seen at all and kept reminding everyone she was serving at her cousin's pleasure.

Another humiliation.

"Yes," she said. "My mother is Mr. Shephard's sister."

"It must have been hard for your family to part with you," the Duchess of Crestwood said. "It's such a long journey, and I hear you will stay with us at least the Season."

Helena hesitated. The subject of her family was not an easy one, and she was searching for a smooth explanation when Uncle Peter snorted out a laugh.

"Her family can do well enough without her," he said, his mouth full of biscuit. "They were happy enough to see her be put to a valuable vocation rather than—"

"I needed a companion and Helena had nothing better to do, so here we are," Charity interrupted, and Helena had never been so happy about anything in her life. Had he truly been about to imply or even outright say what had separated her from her

34

family's good graces?

Suddenly the terrace, with all its lovely spring breezes and beautiful flowers, felt confined. She couldn't help but note how the others at the table stared at her, filling in their own opinion of whatever her uncle was going to say, no doubt. Her mind spun and her hands shook.

"We are very happy you are *all* here," Baldwin's sister said with a warm smile. "And now I see my mother rising from her table. She has some lawn games planned for the remainder of our time together."

Helena moved in a fog, only half-listening as the Duchess of Sheffield made her announcements about lawn games. Then everyone started to rise, shuffling toward the large set of stone steps that led into the garden below. Helena hung back as they did so, staring back over her shoulder at the house. She needed a moment to gather herself. To try to put on that friendly, happy face that was required to survive the endless indignities serving her uncle and cousin required.

So she backed away, happy that her uncle seemed more interesting in prattling on at the Dukes of Donburrow and Crestwood than he was at noticing she'd disappeared. She turned and entered the house, sucking in deep breaths of air as she did so. Blindly, she walked through the parlor and down the hall, turning toward another of the rooms so she might have a better chance of escaping the discovery of whatever servants came to tidy up the veranda from the tea.

As she turned the corner into the room, she came to a sudden stop. This was no parlor where she could have a moment alone. This was the Duke of Sheffield's study, and the man, himself, was seated at a large, mahogany desk across the room, his gaze focused on a letter in his hand. She hadn't even realized he'd left the party, but here he was.

She ought to have turned and run right then and there. Then he'd never know she was there. But she couldn't. She found herself staring at him, at his stern expression, at the way he lifted a hand and ran it through his hair as his lips pressed together.

And her heart fluttered wildly.

He glanced up, and the moment she'd been granted to escape undetected disappeared. His lips parted and he set the letter down as he stood.

"I'm—I'm so sorry," she stammered, staggering away and shaking her head as reality returned. "I shouldn't have intruded."

He lifted a hand. "You have not, Miss Monroe. Please, don't run away."

She swallowed and stopped backing from the room. Less than an hour ago she had felt pushed aside by this man. Now he came around the desk and there was no one in the world other than him.

"I-I didn't know you were a duke that night on the terrace at the Rockford ball," she burst out.

His brow knitted and he stared at her in confusion. "I realized later that *neither* of us made our introductions. I suppose our conversation was too interesting to think of it. Would it have made a difference if you'd known?"

She shifted. "I prattled on rather foolishly, didn't I? And treated you without the deference that the title requires."

He snorted out a laugh. "I have quite enough deference, both false and real, Helena, I assure you."

She blinked. Had he just called her by her given name? He had, for the word hung between them like a caress. She did not correct him. "Still, I shouldn't have been so informal."

"You were charming." He took another step closer, and she couldn't help but catch her breath. He was quite tall, quite confident. It felt like he filled the space, but not in an intimidating way. It was actually almost comforting. "I enjoyed our conversation."

"As did I," she admitted because she could think of no proper lies that would create the distance she so obviously needed.

He tilted his head as he eased to a stop at less than an arm's length from her. He made no move to touch her. Probably best considering the tension that now coursed in the room between them.

"Why did you leave the garden party?" His voice was suddenly rough, low, not accusatory, but undeniable.

She worried her lip a moment. There was no earthly reason for her to tell this man, this stranger, this *duke* who was utterly out of her sphere, the truth. But she felt that very thing on her tongue. A thousand words that explained her reduced position and the discomfort and shame heaped upon her because of it.

"I needed a moment," she said. Not a lie. Not the whole truth. His face lit up with interest as she said it, and she could hardly think or breathe as she continued, "And I took a wrong turn, thinking this was a parlor where I might have a bit of peace."

"Lucky for me," he murmured, his dark brown gaze holding hers firmly.

She swallowed hard. "What about you, Your Grace—"

He flinched. "Baldwin."

"You wish for me to call you *Baldwin*?" she repeated, her voice little more than a squeak that hardly breached even the limited distance between them. "Your—your *given* name?"

"If we are alone, yes. I prefer it. The title is not...comfortable. It never has been." He blinked as if he hadn't meant to say that. "I suppose you're asking why I am not at my own party?"

She nodded, though in truth she'd all but forgotten that question had once been on her tongue.

He ran that same hand through his hair again and she wished she could repeat the action. Feel the short locks against her fingertips. Ascertain if his hair was soft, if it tickled her palm.

"I had a piece of business that came up," he explained. "Something I thought could not wait. Turns out it was..." He trailed off and looked behind him at his desk. "It wasn't what I was hoping for."

She saw the tension on his face. Not the heated kind that so unexpectedly flowed between them, but something less comfortable. Something unpleasant. It drew his lips down in a deeper frown.

"I'm sorry," she said slowly, and wished she were in a position where she could say more. After all, she knew disappointment, she knew regret. She recognized them both. She recognized when a man could use a sympathetic ear.

"You needn't be," he began with a shrug that pushed aside all those emotions he likely hadn't meant to reveal. "It is not your problem, after all."

"That does not mean I'm not sorry that it is yours," she responded.

He tilted his head and the silence stretched between them, not uncomfortable, but also not without tension or heat. He opened his mouth as if he were about to say something to her, but before he could there came a sound from the hallway.

"Blast it all, Helena, where are you?"

Helena squeezed her eyes shut for a beat. "My cousin," she murmured.

"We could shut the door," Baldwin suggested.

Her eyes flew open and she stared at him. He seemed serious. Too serious. And the idea of him reaching behind her and shutting them in alone in his office was tempting beyond measure.

And inappropriate beyond words.

"I can't," she whispered.

More disappointment flowed over his features before he shrugged. "Of course."

She drew a ragged breath, then called out, "I'm here, Charity."

There were footsteps and then Charity appeared in the doorway. "Honestly, Papa is going to have a—oh, Your Grace."

Her tone changed from strict to sweet in nothing more than a word. Charity smoothed her gown and pushed past Helena into Baldwin's office, her hips shimmying with every step. Helena watched his reaction, watched as his gaze slid over her pretty cousin, from her perfect blonde hair to her expensive slippers. Whatever he thought, Helena could not tell. He had shut off the sharing of any emotion.

"Miss Shephard," he said, his tone just as unreadable as his expression. "Good afternoon once again."

"I hope my cousin hasn't been bothering you," Charity said with a glare at Helena that made the heat of a blush flood her cheeks. "She obviously doesn't know her place if she is roaming through your home unattended."

"On the contrary, I was happy to bump into her," Baldwin said. "And just as happy that *you* have come to save me from the distraction that took me from the party. Shall we return together, ladies?"

He looked toward Helena, but before she could respond, Charity sidled up beside him and glided her hand right into the crook of his elbow. "Lead the way, Your Grace," she cooed, batting her pretty blue eyes at him.

He cleared his throat. "Of course."

The pair walked to the door, and Helena stepped aside as they exited the room. She trailed after them, heart throbbing as Baldwin led them back out onto the terrace and down to the garden where the games had already began.

But he looked back as they reached the grass. Right back at her. Their gazes met, held, and she forced a small smile at him. He returned something much the same, and then he released her cousin and returned to the lord of the manor act that he had to play.

But she'd seen something real in him. Something she ought not to have seen. And she would not forget it soon, nor forget the feelings this unattainable man inspired in her.

Baldwin watched from his front step as the last of the carriages pulled away, taking his guests back to where they'd come from. Leaving him in peace, at last. Only he didn't feel peaceful.

"That went well."

He jumped, for his sister Charlotte's voice was right beside him. He didn't even know she had moved so close.

He pivoted toward her with a shrug. "As well as any of these things do."

Charlotte stared at him a moment and then turned. "Ewan, didn't you and Mama want to talk about improvements to the garden back in Donburrow? You even brought a diagram, I think."

Ewan had been standing back, but now he arched a brow at his wife. Then he nodded and held out an elbow to the Duchess of Sheffield. She took it with a warm smile for her much-beloved son-in-law and said, "Oh, excellent, I've been so looking forward to the time I'll spend with you later this summer. If we have all our plans made before then, it will make the visit all the more pleasant. Will you and Charlotte join us, Baldwin?"

"No, for I think I'd like to take a walk with Baldwin," Charlotte answered for him. Her dark green eyes continued to hold his, even and unwilling to accept refusal.

Baldwin knew when he was beaten and held out an elbow. "To the garden, then," he said.

Ewan and the duchess entered the house together, and Baldwin took his sister down the steps and around a pretty path that took them into his garden. Once they were out of earshot, he said, "And does Ewan really wish to talk to Mama about azaleas?"

Charlotte laughed softly. "Yes, he truly did. He really does plan to redesign the garden and Mama has such a talent in that arena. But he also knows when I want an excuse to be alone with my brother."

"And he always gives you what you want," Baldwin mused.

She glanced up at him, and her smile was soft and filled with pleasure. "He does," she said. "The past five months of our marriage have been the happiest of my life. I love him, Baldwin. It makes all the difference in the world."

Baldwin nodded slowly. "I'm very happy for you, then,

Charlotte. I was hard on him during your…well, I suppose we'll call it a courtship, despite how close we've always been. But it's only because I wanted to keep you from grief."

"Is that the same reason you lie to me now?" she asked, releasing his arm as they at last entered the garden. "To keep me from grief?"

He hesitated. Charlotte had been pressing him to reveal his troubles for a long time. Years, probably. He always dodged it. Now he felt even more of a drive to do so. If she told Ewan then everyone in their group of friends would know.

Humiliations galore would follow, even if intentions were the best.

"Lie to you?" he said, keeping his tone light. "You wound me."

He paced away but felt her watching him. Her concern was palpable.

"I'm no fool," she said softly. "Is it so very bad that you can't trust me?"

He pivoted. "You assume there is some heavy secret on my shoulders. Can you not just believe that I am merely a more serious person than my friends and leave it at that?"

She tilted her head. "Dearest brother, I have been a keen observer of your behavior for twenty-five years. You've changed in the last five of them. Since Father died."

He flinched. "Well, how could I not be changed? I became a duke, did I not? There are responsibilities—"

"It's more than that," she interrupted, coming to take his hands. He allowed it, even as he fought to keep his expression neutral. She stared into his face for a moment, then sighed. "Very well, I can see I'm making things worse with my prying rather than better. You know that I love you and that I am here for you if you change your mind."

He nodded before he leaned down to kiss her cheek. "I do know both those things. I appreciate them, I assure you."

Her concern had not left her face, but she smiled regardless. "Let me change the subject then."

"Do!" he encouraged with a laugh as he motioned for her to walk with him.

"Mama seems determined to parade a cadre of ladies before you this Season. So many 'prospects' today that it made my head spin. Have any of them caught your eye?"

Baldwin swallowed as he pictured the one and only lady in attendance who did capture his interest: Helena. When she'd intruded upon him in his office, he had wanted such things. Things his normally very proper brain didn't let him think about. He was a gentleman, raised by a gentleman. One did not think about grabbing ladies and kissing them. Nor of shutting the office door and…well, doing more than merely kiss.

That those impulses reared up in him around Helena was shocking, frankly. It set him on his heels.

"I shall turn the question on you," he said. "You met all my prospects today. Are there any that you could call sister without pulling a face?"

Her expression softened. "I would accept anyone you married, assuming she made you happy."

Baldwin bent his head. Happiness was not in the equation at present. "That doesn't count as a response. You always have an opinion."

"I've known most of your prospects for years," she said slowly. "They're all decent enough people. None have the…the spark that I thought you'd seek. The only stranger in our midst was that American girl, Charity Shephard."

Baldwin swallowed. Here was Charlotte, dancing ever closer to the truth. "She's interesting, I'd say."

Charlotte's eyebrows lifted. "That would be one way of putting it. She's different, but I suppose that comes from being raised in a very different environment than ours."

"You don't like her," Baldwin said flatly, and by his sister's expression he could see he'd struck on the truth.

"Perhaps she'll grow on me," she said with a shrug. "You know who I did like today?"

"Who?" he encouraged.

"Her cousin, Helena."

Baldwin let out his breath softly. Of course. Of course Charlotte would like Helena. Because the universe was patently unfair. "Yes, she's very likeable," he said. "You were seated with her and her family, weren't you?"

"Yes." Charlotte's smile widened. "There's this little spark to her that I cannot help but be attracted to. She comes across as someone who'd be a good friend. Who would fit in with Emma, Meg and Adelaide, too."

These were the wives of his married friends, and Baldwin found himself nodding. He could easily see Helena amongst their ranks. Emma and Adelaide would be attracted to her sweetness, and Meg would love that she was the kind of woman who counted stars without apology.

"Well, she's serving as her cousin's companion," he said, reminding himself as much as informing his sister. "I doubt she could be considered a—a prospect."

Charlotte wrinkled her brow. "I've never known you to be such a snob, Baldwin. Her family back in Boston sounds to be as good as her cousin's. And we've never stood on ceremony in our circles."

Baldwin shook his head. Once again, they were back to a subject he couldn't…wouldn't discuss. "Well, I'm sure she'll find a match if she wishes to do. Why don't we join Mama and Ewan?"

His sister stared at him a moment, but then shrugged. "Certainly, if you'd like to. I suppose we've all had more than enough air today."

She turned toward the terrace and Baldwin fell into step beside her. But even as he tried to refocus, to push aside the topics his sister had broached, he found he kept returning to images of fiery red hair, bright green eyes and a smile that lightened his load.

Images of a woman he could not pursue, no matter how pleasant a thought that was.

CHAPTER FIVE

"We have something to discuss."

Helena looked up from her plate to see her uncle staring at her. She swallowed. "We? Do you mean you and me?"

"All of us," Charity interjected.

Helena fought the urge to sigh and set her napkin aside next to her untouched breakfast plate. "What is it?"

She already knew the answer. But anything to put off the inevitable.

"Charity tells me she found you alone with the Duke of Sheffield yesterday when you snuck away from the party," Uncle Peter said, spearing her with a glare.

Helena glanced at Charity. Of *course* she would run to tattle on her. It was in her nature, encouraged by her father and her late mother to seek out any unfairness or tiny slight she felt against herself, then tell the world about it. It had been that way with Charity since birth, and she rather expected that it would be until the grave.

"I-I didn't sneak away, exactly," Helena said carefully. "I only needed a moment. There were so many people, so many strangers."

He slammed a hand down on the table to interrupt her. "How can I make myself clearer to you, you dolt of a girl? You are here to polish your cousin's diamond, not to call attention to yourself or to try to whore your way into trouble like you did in Boston."

Charity turned her face as tears flooded Helena's eyes, followed by a pain she rarely allowed herself to feel. "That— that isn't what happened in Boston," she whispered, trying to push aside terrifying images. Painful ones. Ones that had changed her life, altered her spirit.

He lifted his brows. "It is what is happening now. You will do your duty, girl. And be happy that we've included you in your cousin's future. That is a far better end for you than you could have had, isn't it?"

Helena swallowed. In truth, he wasn't wrong. Her life with Charity and Uncle Peter might be difficult, but it was nothing compared to what her family had done to her back home.

"Yes," she whispered. "I apologize, Uncle. I won't forget myself again."

He pushed to his feet with a grunt. "Your cousin and I are going out," he snapped. "We will be gone the whole day, so I suggest you think about your actions and ponder your next steps very carefully."

Helena supposed this news was meant to be a punishment to her, but her heart soared even as she kept a somber, reflective expression. "Of course. I understand completely."

"Good." He turned to Charity. "Go upstairs and change into your best dress. We're going on some calls."

Charity sighed and motioned to Helena. "Come on then."

Helena got up and followed her from the room. She was all but bouncing as she did so. She would have a whole day to herself to read and relax, to be free of the oppressive bonds put on her by her position. And perhaps her uncle would be more right than he knew. A day away would likely put her in a better mind to rededicate herself to her duties.

After all, she had no other choice in the matter.

"I beg your pardon, Miss Monroe."

Helena looked up from her book and smiled at her uncle's butler, Aniston. He was rather a kind man—she had noted that he always treated her with the same consideration as he did Charity, despite their disparate positions.

"What is it?" she asked, setting her book aside and rising.

"You have guests, miss."

She drew back. "Guests? Who is it?"

"The Duchesses Abernathe, Crestwood, Northfield and Donburrow," he explained while wringing his hands gently before him.

Her lips parted in shock. "I—oh! That is surprising. I wasn't expecting anyone, certainly not anyone of such stature."

"Shall I tell the ladies you are not in residence?" he asked.

She pondered the question a moment. It was an excuse to hide, to protect herself. But then she thought of the Duchess of Crestwood and of Baldwin's sister, the Duchess of Dunborrow. They'd both been very friendly and kind at the garden party the previous day. They'd know she'd refused them if Aniston returned to say she was not at home.

She didn't want to hurt any feelings, nor incur any more of her uncle's wrath than she already had. She could well imagine his reaction if she sent four duchesses away.

"Of course I am in residence. Will you show them in and send for tea for us if they stay?"

He nodded, and within moments returned with the four ladies. Helena couldn't help but pause as they came into the parlor. They were all so beautiful, though in very different ways. Dark and light, shy and outgoing. Of course, all their gowns were perfection, which made her more conscious of her own worn one that she'd inherited from Charity and had to alter.

"Good afternoon," she said, forcing herself to come forward with a smile. "I'm so sorry if I forgot you were calling."

The Duchess of Donburrow caught her hands, squeezing them gently. "You didn't, dear Helena. We were out shopping together and drove by. It was a very rude thing to do, dropping in on you uninvited, but I so wanted to see you and introduce you to my friends." She motioned to the others. "You know Meg, of course, from my brother's party the other day. This is Emma, Duchess of Abernathe, and Adelaide, the Duchess of Northfield."

Helena swallowed. "Good afternoon to you all. Welcome, though I'm afraid my uncle and my cousin are not home at present to receive you."

To her surprise, the Duchess of Crestwood's eyes lit up. "Oh, such a shame," she said, but there was no mistaking the sarcasm that laced her tone.

The Duchess of Abernathe sent her a side look. "We knew, actually. We were at the apothecary and overheard a friend saying that your uncle was out and about with your cousin making calls. We came because we wanted to see *you*."

"Me?" Helena gasped.

"Yes," the Duchess of Northfield said with a warm smile. "Meg and Charlotte spoke so very highly of you, Emma and I wanted to meet you straight away."

Warmth washed over Helena, both the stinging kind that came from embarrassment and the pleasurable kind that came from joy. She had very much liked Baldwin's sister and the Duchess of Crestwood. That they liked her in return was very nice, indeed.

"I—well, come and sit, Your—Your Graces? Your Grace, Your—"

"Oh dear!" the Duchess of Crestwood interrupted. "That will not do. When we're all in a room together, it is far too confusing to go by title or to Your Grace. We're *friends*, or we shall soon be, I wager. Why don't we go by first names?"

Helena hesitated. Her uncle had drilled the importance of rank into her and her cousin. She'd been taught that those with titles always liked to be called by them, that to do otherwise was considered impertinent, but that had been disproven first by Baldwin and now by these ladies. "I don't know…"

"*We* do!" Adelaide said with a laugh. "It is Emma, Meg, Adelaide and Charlotte, and *you* shall be Helena and that is the end of it!"

Helena laughed along with the other women. It was impossible to do otherwise. She nodded at last. "It will make it easier, I suppose. Please sit. Aniston is bringing tea as we speak."

"Excellent," Charlotte said, coming around to sit in one of the chairs.

They each took their place with Helena back on the settee, flanked by Adelaide and Emma. Emma picked up the book that had slid between the cushions when Helena was interrupted, and smiled.

"Oh, this is a favorite of mine!" she said, thumbing the pages gently. "What part are you on?"

Helena blushed. "Just to where she climbs out the window."

Emma nodded with enthusiasm. "Do you like Lord Evans better or Lord Winter?"

"Lord Winter, obviously. He's quite devilish."

"A girl after all our hearts," Adelaide laughed. "I think we're *all* proof that devilish men are best."

Charlotte folded her arms in mock upset. "My Ewan is only devilish when it is appropriate."

"Your Ewan is a devil in disguise, I think," Meg teased.

Helena watched it all with surprise. She had expected ladies of such rank to be stuffy. These women were anything but. They laughed and teased and she never felt left out of it, even though it was obvious the foursome were fast friends. It was the first time she'd felt comfortable in…well, a very long time.

"But we're not here to talk about devilish husbands," Emma said, blushing prettily. "That is *not* a proper subject, no matter how pleasing it is. We came here to get to know you, Helena."

At that moment, a maid entered and Helena got to her feet to help arrange the sideboard. When the servant had left, she began to pour the tea. She was surprised when Charlotte came and helped her, sweetening as her friends liked and handing out the cups.

"You are under no obligation to answer our brazen

questions," Charlotte reassured her as they returned to the group at last.

Helena shifted under their regard. "I'm not certain you've asked any yet. What is it you'd like to know?"

"Boston is a long way from here," Emma said. "Do you miss home?"

Helena let out a sigh. "In truth, not much. I was not very happy there as of late. I see this as an adventure."

Adelaide smiled. "I like that attitude. Since your name is different, I assume your uncle is…"

"From my mother's side," Helena said with a nod. "He's my mother's older brother. He, er, well, he took me in."

Not exactly true, but far less humiliating than saying what had really happened. She caught Adelaide and Emma exchanging a brief look, and blushed.

"He's brought you to us," Meg said. "So for that, we're grateful. Obviously you and Emma share a love of books. Do you have any other hobbies?"

"I play piano a little. *Very* little and quite poorly."

Emma raised a hand with a laugh. "We could torture a room together, I think!"

Helena shook her head. It was hard to look at the Duchess of Abernathe with her sweet expression and perfect hair and clothes, with her subtle sophistication that seemed to drip from her, and think the lady was not accomplished in every way.

"It is true," Meg said with a teasing wink for Emma. "Once Emma tried to play some of the *Irish Melodies* and…" She dissolved into giggles, along with the other women.

Emma lifted her chin, but though she feigned offense, it was obvious from her sparkling gaze that she found as much humor in it as her friends. "And the cat began to howl. I am not ashamed of it. I thought we made a charming duet."

Helena lifted a hand to cover her own giggles. "The same happened to me. Only it was my uncle's hounds who accompanied me. Until—" She broke off as the amusing memory turned harsher. Uncle Peter had been very angry.

Adelaide eyed her sharply and then smiled, almost with understanding. Swiftly she changed the subject, and for the next hour Helena was enraptured by her four new friends. The women were kind and engaging, funny and friendly. Emma told stories of her precious baby Beatrice, who everyone called Bibi, and Helena thought she caught a glimpse of Meg touching her belly whenever the subject arose. It was all so very comfortable and Helena found she didn't want it to end.

But at last, Charlotte stood and said, "Oh, gracious, we've intruded on your time far more than we should."

Helena followed her to her feet and said, "I assure you there was nothing intrusive about it. I very much enjoyed our tea."

Charlotte gave the others a look and said, "Good. Then I hope you'll come to supper at my home in three days hence."

Helena stared at her, surprised at the invitation. And knowing she could in no way accept it even if she wanted to. But there was no way she could pretend—past today, at least—that she belonged in the world of these women. Nor that her uncle would ever let her take even a tiny place in it.

"I—" she began, shifting with discomfort as she sought a way to refuse without offending a lady she truly liked.

Meg's expression softened, and she stepped up to take Helena's hand. "My dear, it's clear you are uncomfortable and Charlotte would never in the world make you so. Just say whatever you must say and don't fret over consequences that do not exist."

Helena glanced over at Charlotte and found her nodding. She took a deep breath and said, "I'd love to—to join you, of course. More than anything after today. But I couldn't...I couldn't possibly without my...without..."

Emma nodded. "I understand. You couldn't do it without your family."

Charlotte wrinkled her brow. "There is a simply solution to that problem. I shall invite you all, uncle and cousin included. They needn't know it is really *you* all of us wish to spend time with."

Helena stared. "I don't know what it is I've done to inspire your kindness, but it is much appreciated. I can never really speak for my uncle, but I doubt he would dare turn down an invitation from such an important group."

Charlotte smiled. "Then I am happy to trade on Ewan's title. I will send a formal invitation as soon as I arrive home. Do your best to appear shocked and awed by it."

Helena laughed. "I will practice."

They moved into the foyer, where Aniston returned with the hats and gloves. As the duchesses gathered themselves, Charlotte cast Helena one more look. "It might also interest you that my brother will be in attendance to my little gathering."

Helena fought to keep her expression calm at the quiet little explosion that had just gone off in the midst of the foyer. She had no idea why Charlotte would think to specially mention Baldwin to her. All Helena knew was that being around the duke made her...nervous. Fluttery.

"Well, I'm sure my uncle will be very happy to hear that, as well," she managed to choke out. "Thank you again for calling."

The carriage pulled around and the ladies said their final goodbyes, then headed out to the vehicle. Helena stepped out onto the stairs to wave them off, but as she did so, she recognized that her hand was shaking.

And that she was looking forward to seeing Baldwin again even more than she was looking forward to spending time with her new friends.

CHAPTER SIX

Baldwin ran the end of his fountain pen over the row of numbers once again, doing the sum in his head. He frowned and went through the motions again. It was no good. He could add and re-add all he liked, but the problem remained the same.

They were hemorrhaging money and there were still those three debts outstanding, poised over his head like an ever-present guillotine. He dipped his pen in ink and scrawled a number in the field, then shoved the entire pile of papers and writing instruments aside with a curse.

"That is a bad start," Charlotte said as she breezed into his office with a smile on her face. One that was rapidly falling as she looked at him. "Is this not a good time?"

Baldwin jumped to his feet and came around the desk. "Charlotte, I had no idea you'd come to call. My apologies for my bad behavior."

She shook her head as she bussed his cheek. "I insisted on coming to you myself and not being announced. Is there something I can do?"

She nodded to his desk and he glanced over his shoulder, then shook his head. "No, no. Just annoyed with some…" He searched for a lie. "Some information from the tenants out in Sheffield. Nothing that needs your worries."

She wrinkled her brow as if she didn't quite believe him, so he caught her arm and guided her to the fireplace where he motioned for her to sit. "Join me. Will you have sherry?"

"At eleven in the morning?" she asked.

He blinked. He hadn't been thinking about the time. "Ah, my apologies. Of course not. But there must be a reason you called."

"There is," she said, her expression brightening. He was glad to see it. Charlotte was so very happy since her marriage, he didn't want to darken her mood with his troubles. Or have her find out what he'd done to increase them.

"And what is that?" he asked.

"Ewan and I are having a gathering tomorrow. Supper and perhaps some parlor games. We wanted you to join us."

Baldwin leaned back. "*Ewan* wanted to have a gathering?"

"He's always been reclusive, of course, but Baldwin, he is truly trying to come out of his shell since our marriage." She smiled broadly. "All his talk of coming into what he perceives as 'my' world and no longer hiding because of his mutism is...well, it's true."

Baldwin watched her as she spoke, saw her joy at Ewan's behavior. And his smile was very real as he said, "You give him the strength, I think."

"I hope so," she sighed. "He certainly gives me mountains of the same in return. So while I wouldn't say he is *excited* about a gathering, he did suggest it."

He lifted his brows. "That's wonderful."

She nodded. "I must encourage it. Honestly, it will mostly be friends."

There wasn't something about the way she said the last sentence that made Baldwin examine her more closely. He knew his sister very well and he could tell when she was plotting. Right now Plotting Charlotte sat across from him, trying to look sweet as sugar and innocent as a newborn lamb.

"*Mostly?*" he repeated in a warning tone.

She shrugged. "Yes. Mama will be there. James and Emma, Simon and Meg, Graham and Adelaide. Matthew will be there. I'm trying to coax Hugh, as well. Have you spoken to him of late? I saw him at Mattigan's Bookshop and he—"

"Charlotte!" Baldwin interrupted. "What does mostly mean?"

She pursed her lips. "You needn't be so cross about it. Aside from our friends, we have invited...the...Americans."

Baldwin froze. "The Americans," he repeated slowly. "You mean Mr. Shephard and his daughter. What is her name? Cora? Cassandra?"

"Charity. And they are bringing along Charity's cousin, Helena Monroe," Charlotte added, and there was no hiding how she watched him as she said Helena's name.

It was almost impossible for him not to react to the same. *Helena.* He'd been thinking of her for days, since his garden party. Since she'd found him in his study and made him want to do incredibly scandalous things to her.

"In truth," his sister continued. "We only wanted Helena, but Charity and her father come along with her, so sacrifices must be made, it seems."

Baldwin glared at her. "You only wanted Helena."

"Why wouldn't we?" she said with a light laugh. "She is a delight, Baldwin—have you had a chance to talk to her?"

"Very little," he said as he pushed to his feet and paced away. "When have *you* had the chance?"

"We sat together at your party a few days ago, of course. Then all the duchesses were on an outing and we stopped by to say hello. Had the most marvelous tea and a lovely chat with her."

Baldwin shook his head slowly. Of course he was not opposed to the idea of Helena becoming friends with his sister and the wives of his friends. Only he was aware of the ulterior motives his sister was capable of concocting. Especially when she had no idea of the circumstances he was in. "Charlotte, why are you so invested in this?"

She leaned back with a falsely insulted expression. "Invested? Whatever do you mean, Baldwin?"

"'Whatever do you mean?'" he repeated in a singsong

voice. "You are meddling. You've thrown this girl in my path more than once."

Now Charlotte actually *did* look offended. "Thrown her? It seems to me you've done a fine job of stepping into her path."

He folded his arms, trying not to think of his offer to close the study door when he and Helena were together. That was certainly putting himself in her path, there was no denying it. At least to himself.

"That is an argument of semantics," he snapped.

"No, it isn't," she said with a laugh that ignored his ill humor. "Do you *like* her?"

Baldwin hesitated, long enough that he would wager she had her answer. She'd always been able to read him so well. "I have hardly talked to her," he repeated, exhaustion in his voice and in his body. "Once at the Rockford Ball, twice at the garden party. I don't like or dislike her. I don't know her."

But he wanted to. Fiercely.

Charlotte's expression grew worried and she moved toward him. She reached for his hands and held them gently in her own as she stared up into his face. "You are so troubled, Baldwin. Please, please talk to me."

He shook his head and glanced away from her. "It is…complicated."

"Father died years ago," she said softly. "It's been complicated ever since. I've seen you change, Baldwin. I've watched you grow more and more serious, more and more concerned. I'm not so stupid that I don't make the connection between his death and your slow descent into worry and regret."

He drew a deep breath. "I would never say you were stupid, my dear. Your sharp tongue and quick wit are too undeniable when turned on me. But you don't…know."

Her face twisted a little. "Because you won't tell me. Nor anyone else."

He sensed the frustration she was trying to rein in, trying to soften in an effort to empathize with his situation. In an effort to uncover the whole of it.

He hated himself for causing that emotion, but the other option was to crush her down to her very soul. To make her doubt what she'd known about her father, about him.

"I love you," he said instead, leaning down to kiss her forehead.

She was clearly fighting to stay on topic, but at last she sighed. "I know that. And I hope you know that my interference, such as it is, is also born from love."

"I do," he said, and meant it. "I will come tomorrow, though I think you should let go of any notions you have in your head about me and Miss Monroe. She is charming, as you say, but there is no future there. I have other obligations that I must fulfill."

There was a flash of disappointment over her face, but she wiped it away. "Whatever you say, Baldwin. You are certainly well capable of making your own decisions. We look forward to seeing you tomorrow. Now I must go—I have to make a stop to call on Mama and then Ewan is expecting me."

Baldwin barely stifled a sigh of relief that she would go. He loved seeing her, but she laid bare the problems in his life, without even meaning to. He followed her into the foyer where he kissed her cheek. But as she turned to go, he said, "And why don't you let me talk to Brighthollow?"

"If you think Hugh will listen to you and accept our invitation, I shall do just that. Send word of his response, though, so I may plan accordingly."

He nodded and she squeezed his hand one more time before she hurried to her carriage and left him in a cloud of sweet perfume and bitter worries. About the future. About the past. And about a woman he really couldn't have.

Hugh Margolis, Duke of Brighthollow, looked up from the letter on his desk and smiled as Baldwin stepped around his butler and into the room. Baldwin returned the expression even as he studied his old friend's face.

Brighthollow had always been stern. There was a hardness to him, an edge that none of their other friends had. Of course, it was bound to be there. He'd been duke the longest, taking on the title when he was just seventeen, after his father and mother died in a terrible accident. He'd been left with a sister in his charge, twelve years his junior.

Brighthollow had grown up very quickly.

"You look like hell," Hugh said with a chuckle.

Baldwin glared at him. "Thank you. I appreciate the kind concern, you lout."

"Come in, sit down, have a drink. I was happy to receive your letter and happier still to receive *you*." Hugh moved to the sideboard as he spoke and splashed scotch into a glass that he handed over.

"The same from my side," Baldwin said as they lifted their glasses. "There are fewer and fewer in our ranks who are bachelors—we must stick together."

He had meant the quip as a joke, but Hugh's expression darkened and he took a deep sip of his drink before he said, "Ah yes, our friends who are deep in the throes of true love." He rolled his eyes.

The harsh words made Baldwin examine his face more closely. There was more than Hugh's usual seriousness in his eyes. There was…anger there. Darkness.

"Are you so opposed to true love?" Baldwin asked, choosing each word carefully.

Hugh shrugged. "I'm certain some find it and one cannot find fault with our friends' choices of wives thus far, but…"

He trailed off, and Baldwin leaned forward. "But?"

"Not everyone is what they seem," Hugh finished. "I have doubts that something so flippant as true love can last."

Baldwin flinched. "I cannot argue the idea that some people are not what they seem." He shifted. "Charlotte said she saw you at Mattigan's."

Hugh lifted his gaze from his drink. "Yes, I saw her yesterday, I think it was. She mentioned it to you?"

"Yes, and that she was attempting to coax you to supper tomorrow with the group and some outside friends."

"I'm not in much of a humor to be around people, I'm afraid."

Baldwin chuckled. "She mentioned *that*, too."

Hugh pushed to his feet. "If I offended her—"

"You didn't," Baldwin said. "Worried her, I think is more accurate, and sitting here with you, I must admit you are worrying me a bit, too."

Hugh speared him with a glance. "So this isn't a social call, but a fishing expedition."

"It won't be a fishing expedition if you don't make me fish," Baldwin said, getting up, too. "Do you want to talk about what is troubling you?"

Hugh scrubbed a hand over his face and the anger there turned to worry, even fear. "Just some...some trouble with Lizzie."

Baldwin drew back. Lizzie was only sixteen, not even out yet. She and Hugh had always gotten along, the girl looked on him as a father rather than a brother. For all intents and purposes, he had been. She was so young when she lost her parents.

"Is there anything I can do?"

"No," Hugh said, his tone growing dark again. "I have— I've managed it as best I can. She's safely back in Brighthollow now."

Baldwin tilted his head. "Safely?"

"What about you?" Hugh said, ignoring the question. "You have been moping around for quite some time. Would you like *me* to pry into the details of your troubles?"

Baldwin frowned. "No," he said at last.

"I'm sure the others are pressing you on it. That's what they do, after all, and they mean well. But I know better than others that some secrets should not be discussed or exposed. I wouldn't dare to bother you about them. If you see fit to talk about what's troubling you, you will. I only ask the same courtesy from you. At least with each other, we can be untroubled."

Baldwin shifted. The idea of not having to hide or pretend to avoid prying questions was certainly attractive on some level. But Hugh's coldness bothered him.

Still, he held up both hands in surrender. "If you don't wish to speak, we won't speak. But what shall I tell Charlotte about her party?"

Hugh dipped his head. "I've always admired your sister, of course. And I adore Ewan, for he is impossible not to adore. But I...I can't be with people right now. Look at me—you see what I am at present. Give me a few weeks of peace and I promise I'll be of a better mind to see friends."

Baldwin nodded. "Very well. I will make an excuse that she will not press about."

Relief flowed over Hugh's expression and he smiled once more. "Good. Very good. Now what say we play a game of billiards?"

Baldwin grinned and followed his friend from the room. But even as their talk shifted to more benign and less troublesome topics, he couldn't help but feel troubled. For Hugh, yes, for it was clear something terrible weighed on his mind.

But also for himself. Because in Hugh's darkness, he feared he saw his own future. A future where his secrets ate away at his heart and eventually turned him into someone he did not wish to be.

CHAPTER SEVEN

Helena pulled the delicately stitched gown tight across Charity's slender shoulders and went to work on buttoning the long line of pearls along her back. This was something her cousin's maid could have done, of course, but Charity had asked for her.

And Helena had no way to refuse. So she swallowed her humiliation at the way Charity's maid had glared at her, and did her best to play the role of servant.

Not that Charity seemed to notice. She had been chattering nonstop since Helena entered the room a quarter of an hour before.

"But Papa is set on a duke," she continued, and for the first time Helena lifted her gaze and attended to Charity's words.

"It is the highest title until one gets to the princes," Helena said, hoping she sounded light and disinterested in the subject. She was anything but. Dukes were of interest to her. Well, one duke. One who would be in attendance tonight.

"Well, he looked into princes, too," Charity said with a shrug that yanked the buttons from Helena's fingers. "There are no good prospects available."

"Hmmm, so a duke it is," Helena muttered as she went back to her work.

"There will be dukes aplenty tonight. Though many of then are already married, which seems such a waste. Did you know that the group of them have a *club* of some kind?"

Helena swallowed. "Do they? Where did you hear that?"

"When we went on our calls the other day. I was bored almost to tears—the English are so stuffy. But you must have had it worse, Helena. Having to stay here and *read*?"

Helena stifled a smile. Not only did her cousin not understand in the slightest that she enjoyed reading, but she had not mentioned the call she had received from The Duchesses, as she now thought of them. None of the servants had done so either, so her afternoon with Emma, Meg, Adelaide and Charlotte had remained her lovely secret.

"I managed," she said, finishing the buttoning at last and moving to examine her cousin. No one could find fault with her clothing, certainly. Uncle Peter made sure of that, for he had provided her with a ridiculous allowance for gowns.

Helena couldn't help but glance at her own dress. It was serviceable enough, styled to attend a party like tonight's. But she would not stand out in a plain dark green gown with no flourishes. Not that she needed to. She was not meant to capture the attention of a duke, after all.

"You look lovely. Shall I call Perdy to do your hair?"

Charity arched a brow. "I want to talk to you. You do it."

Helena stared at her for a beat. She could not tell if Charity acted this way out of a flare of power or if she were truly so selfish that she was oblivious to the position she put Helena into. Of course, the purpose behind her demands mattered little. Helena had to obey them one way or another.

"Very well, though I doubt I'll do as well as your maid," she said, and barely contained her sigh as she slid a few pins between her lips and caught up Charity's brush and comb.

"Still, it isn't only dukes," Charity said, picking up almost at the same point where she'd left off a moment before. "Father isn't laying off the others, no matter what he says. He made me call on the Earl of Grifford two days ago, did I tell you that?"

Helena shook her head and mumbled around the pins, "No, I don't think that name came up."

"Oh, Helena," Charity said with a sigh. "He is...*old*."

Helena swirled a few strands of hair up and slid a pin into place. "How old?"

"Twenty years my senior," Charity replied. She pulled a face. "I mean, he *is* titled. And I'll admit he isn't entirely awful. He's rather dashing, actually, for a man of his years. But still."

For not the first time, Helena actually felt a twinge of pity for her cousin. Charity had almost as few choices about her future as Helena did. And while Charity might be frivolous and occasionally even unkind, she was not, at her core, a terrible person. She had simply been spoiled; Helena had watched it for years. And for a person accustomed to having whatever she wanted, being turned into a bartering chip must have been quite the shock to the system.

"Well, it sounds as though Uncle Peter has dukes on the mind, so perhaps he only sees Lord Grifford as a standby."

"Yes, I suppose." Charity's bottom lip poked out in a pout for a moment before she straightened up. "There will be a few eligible men there. The Dukes of Sheffield and Tyndale, he says. I haven't met Tyndale yet, though I've heard he's rather handsome. A bit broody, according to gossip. But Sheffield is *very* handsome."

Helena nearly choked on the pins between her lips and withdrew them before she spoke again. "I suppose no one could deny that he is."

"Oh, come, Helena," Charity snapped. "You obviously think he is or you wouldn't have arranged to find yourself alone with him."

Helena gaped. "I did not *arrange* for anything! As I've told you and Uncle Peter at least a dozen times, I merely took a wrong turn and found myself in the man's study! It was a mistake, that is all."

Charity didn't look entirely convinced. "Perhaps. But I would advise you to be careful, Helena. Papa will not be...*pushed*."

Helena frowned. "I-I don't know what you mean."

Except she did. She knew her uncle was not fond of her. He had brought her here because he was cheap and wanted a companion he didn't have to pay. But if she stepped out of the role he intended for her, she knew there would be consequences.

Charity rose to her feet with a shrug. "If you don't do anything wrong, there will be nothing to account for, I suppose." She leaned closer to the mirror, turning to admire herself from each side. "Well, I look very pretty despite your reduced skills with hair. I'll catch a duke yet. If not Sheffield, then perhaps his friend or one of the others. They're all the same, at any rate."

She flounced past Helena and out the door. When she was gone, Helena let out a deep sigh as she stared at herself in the mirror.

"No," she whispered. "They are most definitely not."

Then she followed Charity on the way to the next step on her journey. One she hoped for her own sake would not put her too much in the path of a man who was entirely out of her reach.

If Helena had hoped to stay out of the path of the Duke of Sheffield, her dreams were dashed the moment she arrived at Charlotte and Ewan's home. As their party mounted the steps, with her trailing behind her uncle and cousin, there he was in the foyer with his family to greet them. Her heart, apparently disconnected from all the promises her mind had made to her, skipped a beat like she was the heroine in one of her books.

It was not an unpleasant sensation. She watched as Charlotte and Ewan shook hands with her family. When Helena reached her, the other woman pulled her in for a brief hug.

"We're so very happy to have you!" Charlotte gushed. "You remember Donburrow, yes?"

Helena turned and looked up and up to meet the eyes of the strapping and extremely handsome duke. He smiled, a warm and welcoming expression, and then signed something, which

Charlotte translated as, "You are very welcome, Miss Monroe. My wife has claimed you as a friend and she is never wrong when she judges character."

Helena blushed, not just at the warm compliment, but at the very act of being present with Charlotte and Ewan. They stood so close to each other, their connection on display not just openly, but proudly. Even their language, the one that bridged Donburrow to the rest of the world, was something very intimate. She found herself briefly jealous of her new friend and the love she had found.

She smiled at him and forced herself to say, "I'm very pleased to be here, Your Grace. Thank you for having us."

She moved on to the next in line, Baldwin's mother, the Duchess of Sheffield. Her uncle had just left the lady, and he shot Helena a curious look that made her stomach tighten. Charlotte's warm welcome had obviously sparked his interest. She might have to confess to her friend that she had not told her uncle about their meeting.

What Charlotte's response to that would be was certainly bound to be interesting.

"Good evening, Miss Monroe," the Duchess of Sheffield said, taking her hand gently. "How very happy we are to have you join us."

Helena swallowed hard as she examined the lovely woman before her. Baldwin had her eyes, warm and dark and brown. But like she had observed in the son, his mother also seemed…troubled. What was it that made both of them so anxious?

"Good evening, Your Grace," she said as she pushed her curiosity aside. It had no place with this stranger who owed her nothing. To the duchess, she was hardly more than a servant and she would do well to recall that, whether Charlotte and her friends were open to her or not.

And that left Baldwin. Donburrow's butler was already escorting her uncle and cousin away to a parlor for before supper drinks. And the others in the line had started to move behind them, chatting together as they walked.

She was, for a brief moment, alone with Sheffield.

He stared down at her, his serious face searching hers, for what she didn't know. But heat flooded her cheeks at his intense perusal.

"Good evening, Your Grace," she managed to croak out.

He arched a brow. "Helena. I'm glad you came."

"How does one refuse an invitation from the Duchess of Donburrow?" she said with a light laugh.

"One doesn't," he conceded, and his face finally relaxed into a smile. "A fair point."

He hesitated and then held out his elbow to her. She caught her breath. A duke escorting a lady's companion could not be proper, but refusing that same duke seemed even more ill-mannered. So she reached out and slid her hand into the crook of his arm.

The reaction was immediate. Heated. Unexpected. It was the first time they'd touched, and awareness shot through her as his body heat wound through her. He smelled of that same heat, a leathery scent that made her stomach flip and her legs tremble. And his arm—good God, it was strong. She gripped what felt like a slab of steel and never in her life had she felt so…safe.

She blinked as they entered the parlor, and released him immediately. That was not right. Not good. Not proper.

And certainly it had no end that she could look forward to. Baldwin was seeking a bride amongst ladies. She was a servant in the best light. In the worst…well, he'd never know about that. Still, it precluded her from his attentions.

"Thank you," she stammered, and started across the room away from him without looking back. She walked blindly, trying to find some quiet corner where she could hide until she was called upon by her cousin. A place where she could calm her racing heart and carefully destroy all the inappropriate thoughts that were plaguing her.

Instead, she heard Meg's voice through the soft sounds of the group. "Helena!"

She turned toward her, unable not to smile when Meg was beaming at her, motioning her to join her and her husband and another handsome man. She stepped to them, working hard to keep a serene expression.

"Good evening, Meg and Your Grace."

Meg's husband waved his hand. "Not with that, thank you. If she gets to be Meg, I get to be Simon."

Helena boggled. "I truly do not understand your group. I was told very strictly by my uncle never to be too informal with those who held title. And yet I have been told to call everyone by their first names. If you are not careful, I shall find myself beheaded when I call your prince regent George."

Simon laughed. "Oh no, my dear, you must call him Prinny. We all do."

"I suppose we are more informal than some," the other man in their small group said. "Probably because the men of our circle have been friends far longer than any of us even thought about title. Simon has always been Simon to me. When he's Your Graced, it makes my teeth hurt."

"May I present Miss Helena Monroe to you?" Meg said with a smile. "That is, assuming you have not already met the Duke of Tyndale."

"Or Matthew, if we are being informal," the gentleman said as he caught Helena's hand and raised it for a brief kiss across her gloved knuckles. "And we had not yet met, but I've heard a great deal about you, Miss Monroe."

Helena blinked. They were all so kind. She felt so welcomed. It was lovely and strange all at once.

"Your Grace," she offered. "Gracious, it *is* difficult when there are a group of you, isn't it? I suppose I can see how much easier using first names would be."

"Quite right," Matthew said. "Though if calling me by my Christian name is too bothersome, I also accept Tyndale."

"Perhaps that would be best," Helena said with a blush. "I can only imagine what my uncle would say if he knew Baldwin and all his friends had asked me to call them by their first names."

She heard the words as they exited her mouth and it took everything in her not to slap her hand over her lips. Especially when Tyndale's eyebrow arched ever so slightly at her slip.

But before she had to say anything more, the butler appeared at the doorway, ringing a little bell to indicate their supper was served. The rest started to walk out, and she waited to follow, but to her surprise, Tyndale offered her an arm.

"Charlotte tells me you and I will be seated next to each other tonight. May I take you in?"

She nodded, for there was no other answer, and took his arm. But as they moved to depart the room, she couldn't help but notice that Baldwin was watching them, even as he took her cousin's arm. And he did not seem overly pleased by what he saw.

Helena caught herself staring down the table at Baldwin for the tenth time since supper had started, and forced herself to focus on her plate. She had no right to look at him. No right to wonder what Charity was talking to him about. In a perfect world, at least for her family, he would marry her cousin.

A thought that turned her stomach.

"You look troubled, Miss Monroe."

She jerked her head up to look at Tyndale and found him staring at her closely. She shook her head immediately. "Oh no, of course not, I—"

He leaned in. "I know trouble, Miss Monroe there is no use denying it."

She cleared her throat and shrugged. "I suppose we all have troubles."

His gaze slipped up the table. "I suppose we all do."

She followed his gaze and frowned. Baldwin's expression was perfectly acceptable as he listened to her cousin prattle on incessantly, but there was something to his eyes. Something worried and distant.

She shook her head. "Do you know what troubles *him*?"

Tyndale leaned back in his chair. "You seem to know my friend very well after such a short acquaintance. To call him by his first name, to see that there is something in his eyes that doesn't seem…right."

She caught her breath and looked at Tyndale again. He was observing her with a expression that could not be denied. But it was kind, just as he seemed to be very kind.

"I didn't know who he was the first night I met him," she found herself saying and there was relief in saying anything real at all after all the weeks with her uncle and Charity. "I'm sure he thought me very foolish. But he was very…attentive. And I admit I haven't experienced that in a long time. But now I'm being too forward."

"I asked the question," Tyndale said with a shake of his head. "I was interested in the answer, after all." He seemed to consider her for a moment, then he added, "You asked why he's troubled. I don't know. He doesn't share much. He used to, once upon a time. But since his father's death…well, it changed him."

She tried not to look at Baldwin. "I suppose it would have to. He bears a great deal of responsibility."

"Perhaps more than we know," he mused. "I wish he had a friend he could turn to, but he denies his troubles to all close to him. If he could just say those troubles out loud, I wonder if it would help."

Helena pondered the suggestion. She had to believe it was true. Sometimes she wanted to scream her own troubles from the rafters. Sometimes she longed for a confidante that would hear her, just *hear* her.

The servants cleared the last of the dessert plates away and Helena rose with the others. Matthew smiled at her as he offered his arm a second time. She blushed in response. "I hope I wasn't out of line."

He shook his head. "Not at all."

He took her from the dining room and down a long hall to the parlor where the night had begun. Tables had been placed in the room for games, and a fire burned brightly with a screen positioned for shadow puppets later.

As Matthew released her, he squeezed her hand. "Thank you for the company, Miss Monroe. I very much enjoyed our talk during supper."

Helena nodded, for she had to. Up until the end, it had been very pleasant. Tyndale was a fine companion. She just didn't...want to be near him like she did with Baldwin. Not that either man was in her sphere.

He walked away, and she drew a deep breath at her first moment alone that night. Her cousin slid over to Tyndale as she did, sidling up to him to talk. Her father was close at hand, so Helena didn't feel her duties as companion would be required. She walked to the window and stood there, staring out at the inky night.

"Hello."

She stiffened at the sound of Baldwin's voice, now just at her elbow. Turning, she gave him the brightest smile she could manage when her heart was throbbing. "Your Grace."

He smiled back, but once again she saw that flicker of worry in his stare. Along with something darker, more heated. Her stomach fluttered in response, and she sought some topic, any topic, to make this odd attraction ease a little.

"Your sister seems vastly contented," she burst out.

Baldwin stared at her another beat, then his gaze slid across the room to Charlotte. She was standing beside Ewan, chatting with Emma and James.

"She is," he said, his tone a little faraway. "And I am glad of it. She has not had an easy time. Her first marriage was arranged and I think rather empty. But Ewan is her first and greatest love."

"Is he?" she asked, and looked at the couple.

Baldwin's smile was soft. "She loved him from the time she was seven, I think, and he not much older."

"What kept them apart?" she asked, then shook her head. "Gracious, I am spending this entire evening being entirely inappropriate in what I say. I apologize, Your Grace."

He glanced at her. "Well, I don't know what inappropriate things you said earlier that require absolution. I suppose you'd have to take that up with...I presume Tyndale." There was something brittle in his tone as he said his friend's name. "But I am not offended by the question and I doubt Charlotte would be, either. She and Ewan are open about such things. It isn't as if his mutism is a secret."

She blinked. "I see."

"Charlotte didn't care, of course," Baldwin said. "But Ewan resisted for a long time and nearly lost her. Twice."

Helena drew in a long breath. "It is good he didn't. That they could overcome the walls between them. Some barriers are not so easy to surmount."

Baldwin's expression changed a fraction and he nodded, suddenly very solemn. "Indeed, they are not. But they are good for each other. Certainly, I don't have to—to worry with her so well matched."

Helena glanced at him. Once again she was struck by how forlorn he sounded. Oh, it was clear he was happy for his sister, but he couldn't hide that slightly wistful quality to his voice.

She swallowed hard, her empathy for whatever was troubling him stronger than anything else in that moment. "You seem...troubled," she said. "Would you like to—to walk with me?"

He blinked down at her. "Isn't that my place, to ask you to walk?"

She caught her breath as the impertinence of her suggestion registered with her. "I'm sorry. If you don't want to—" She moved to step away, but he reached out and caught her elbow.

"Will you walk with me, Miss Monroe?"

His voice was so low, almost hypnotic, and she found herself nodding. "Yes," she whispered.

He smiled and took her arm. As they moved toward the

door, he glanced over his shoulder. "Good," he said. "They're all so busy, they do not even notice our departure. That means no awkward looks or explanations."

She felt her smile fall a fraction. Although she was happy for the same reasons he was, she didn't like the idea that he felt he had to sneak away with her. But then, why wouldn't he? She was not, after all, the kind of woman one courted.

And she had to remember that, even if touching him made her heart pound harder and her life seem a little brighter.

CHAPTER EIGHT

"Where will we walk?" Helena asked when the silence between them had stretched too long. She tried to keep a bright tone.

Baldwin continued to lead her through the winding halls. "Charlotte and Ewan have the prettiest garden in the back," he said. "With a fountain that I've heard the Regent himself tried to finagle away when Ewan first inherited his title. He kept it because Charlotte once said she liked it. That was a long time before they married."

Helena smiled as he led her out the front door and around a path to the garden. In the moonlight, everything seemed soft and almost dreamlike, from the perfectly groomed hedges to the pretty stone benches and the lanterns that hadn't been lit since there had been no anticipation that guests would sneak away outside.

"You really have known him a long time."

He nodded. "Yes, we have. Matthew's family was very close to ours, and Ewan was his cousin and ultimately a ward to Matthew's family. We used to spend all number of summers together."

"And that is how you founded your duke club?" she asked, thinking of Charity's statement earlier in the night.

He glanced at her. "Heard of that, have you?"

She laughed. "It is a fact that sticks out in one's mind."

He sighed, but it was one of pleasure rather than sadness. "It is true, our little circle of friends are all dukes. Or all will be—Kit…er, the Earl of Idlewood has not yet inherited. I believe you may have met him at my tea last week."

She nodded. "I do remember him and his father. Very kind."

"They are." Baldwin's frown drew deeper, then he seemed to shake his melancholy away. "But it wasn't the three of us who formed it. That would be James, Simon and Graham. They just dragged us all along."

"You're all so close," Helena said with a shake of her head as she thought of the men. The ones she'd seen together were almost like brothers. "I envy that."

Baldwin expression tightened, but before she could ask him about it, he brought her through one last turn in the hedge maze and she caught her breath. There, in the middle of the garden, was a gorgeous marble fountain of a half-clothed Greek lady pouring water from a pitcher.

Helena stepped away from Baldwin and toward the bubbling beauty before her. "Oh, it's lovely. Her face is so…so enchanting."

"Yes." His voice came softly. "It is."

Heat flooded her cheeks, and she didn't dare turn back for fear she might find him looking at her, not the statue. And if she did, fearing what she might do next. Out here, in the quiet dark, in the soft moonlight, anything seemed possible.

"You miss your friends at home," he said, a statement, not a question.

She continued to look at the statue, though her pleasure in it faded a fraction. "Why do you say that?"

"Because you said you envied my close friendships. So I assumed you must be longing for your own." He stepped up next to her and stared up at the fountain lady's perfectly carved face. Still, she felt his tension. His…waiting.

She swallowed. "I *did* have a circle of friends in Boston," she said, and her eyes stung with sudden tears. "But we—we grew apart in recent years."

She could still recall her best friend giving her the cut direct after her fall. It was a moment she would never forget.

He faced her, his expression suddenly curious. "I suppose that happens," he said softly. "As our lives change."

He was too close now. Too close and too warm in the cool late spring air. She found herself leaning toward him, her body doing what it pleased rather than what was prudent. She caught herself and stepped away.

To her surprise, he followed, closing the distance she had created. Her throat felt like it was tightening and her world began to spin as she stared up into his handsome face. His unattainable and oh-so-very handsome face.

"Baldwin," she squeezed out.

He muttered something beneath his breath and then he reached out, catching her arm and drawing her up against him. His chest was rock solid and her body molded to it like it had been made to do so. She could have pulled away, probably should have, but instead she reached up to grip his forearms, anchoring herself in whatever way she could.

His mouth lowered, torturously slowly, and then she felt his warm breath stir on her lips. She gasped, and it was in that moment that he claimed her mouth. What started as a gentle kiss rapidly spun out of control. His arms came around her, pulling her even closer, and his tongue stroked inside her mouth.

Her world stopped. Ceased to exist. It was replaced only by sensation. Of his hard body against her soft one, of the taste of him, of the smell of his skin. He drove his tongue inside of her with finesse and the perfect combination of dominating demand and gentle coaxing.

She couldn't help but relax. It had been ages since she was kissed, and never like this. Never so...thoroughly. She opened and met his tongue with her own. He made a harsh noise deep in his throat and his hips bumped hers.

She arched against him, lifting to wrap her arms around his neck as she fought for purchase, fought to control, fought to get closer somehow.

But just as suddenly as he had taken her in his arms, he pulled away. He steadied her, then paced off several steps, running his hands through his hair. She watched him, bereft and confused and a tiny bit grateful for his discretion when she'd had none.

"I'm bloody sorry, Helena," he said at last, turning to face her.

Everything seemed almost magical in the moonlight and her heart stuttered with a longing she had never felt before. One that made her braver than she was. She clenched her hands before her, worrying them as she whispered, "Are you? I suppose it would be very wanton of me to tell you I am not."

His eyes went wide and dilated, desire slashing across his angled face. "No, it would be honest." He bent his head. "Honesty is a valuable commodity. One I am sadly lacking."

She stared at him, confused and intrigued. "I cannot imagine that you are not honorable or honest."

He barked out a humorless laugh before he turned away. "No one can imagine it. That is how I've gotten away with everything for so damned long. And here I am, standing in my sister's garden, practically seducing you in front of the lady fountain and you have *no* idea of who I am."

Helena could not deny how she was brought in by his pain. By his struggle that was so obvious in every tense muscle in his body. She moved toward him, stepping around so that he couldn't avoid looking at her. She reached out, hesitant, and took one of his clenched hands in her own.

"What is it?" she whispered. "Can't you tell me?"

He seemed to ponder that a moment, then he nodded. "If I'm going to accost you in the garden and then pull away, I suppose you deserve to know why." He hesitated, and she watched all the color drain from his cheeks. Then he pulled his hand from hers and said, "What you must understand, Helena, is that I have *nothing*."

Baldwin felt the words coming from his mouth, words that had remained unspoken for so many years. And yet he couldn't stop them. He looked at this woman, this lovely woman who fascinated him, and he *wanted* to tell her the truth. He *needed* her to understand why what they'd just done, that stunning kiss, was impossible.

Perhaps he needed to remind himself, as well.

He watched for her reaction, but her expression remained passive, open, accepting rather than judging, and it spurred him on. Not that he could have stopped. Saying it out loud had opened floodgates he'd been bracing against for years.

"No one knows," he continued, moving to sit down hard on the bench across from the fountain. "Not even my mother understands the full extent of the damage to our position, though she is aware of some of it."

Helena took a place beside him. "How did it happen?"

He winced. "*There* is a story."

"You needn't tell me if you don't want to," she said. She reached over and covered his hand with hers. "I'm a stranger, after all."

"After that kiss, I'd say you're more than that," he mused, watching her pale fingers tangle with his. "Here it is, the bottom line of it: my father loved us, I know that is true, but he was selfish. He gambled and he lost. I used to watch him do it with this pit in my stomach. But he was always assuring, always implying that we had more than enough for his foolish decisions not to matter. And when he died—"

He cut himself off with a shake of his head. She nodded slowly. "You discovered the truth."

"Yes," he whispered. "I was already mourning the father I loved, weighed down by grief and responsibility, and then I started finding the ledgers."

"Ledgers?" she repeated.

"Dozens of them, all designed to hide one lie or another, one debt or another." He almost choked on the words. "For six months, as I went through the contents of his office, every single day brought some new nightmare. The creditors were calling and I was in a chess match with a dead man. Every move took me closer to my doom."

"It must have been devastating," she said.

He nodded. "Utterly. But I...I made it worse, Helena. *I* did."

"How?" Her brow wrinkled.

"One of the men my father owed money to, he approached me with a bargain. More gambling to clear the debt. I was against it. By then any stomach I had for the idea was long turned. But I felt I had no choice, so I did so—and I won. That small debt was cleared. It was exhilarating."

He stopped talking and bent his head as shame flooded him. He couldn't say the next, he never had. Not to his mother, not to anyone.

Helena brushed a lock of hair from his forehead. "You gambled more," she said softly, filling in the things he could not bring himself to say. "You tried to fix the damage using the same tools your father had to make it. And I assume it failed."

He nodded without looking at her. "Yes. Though I did clear a few debts, I also incurred more. I stopped after a few months, but the damage was done. By him. By me."

Her breath went out in a shuddering sound that mimicked the one inside his head at all times. "It must be terrible for you."

He dared to look up at last and found her staring back at him. She was care and empathy and support personified. But he wasn't finished yet.

"I'm telling you this, not for your sympathy," he said slowly. "But because I must. I am not the kind of man who goes around kissing young ladies in a garden. I would normally not be so reckless, but the moment I saw you on the terrace at the ball, I was drawn to you. When I look at you I want...well, I simply *want*. But there are still outstanding debts I cannot even find and a future that can be fixed in only one way. So I...I can't pursue what I want. I must do what I need to do, no matter how much I don't want to."

Her eyes widened slightly, and she nodded. "You must marry for money."

He wanted to howl when she said it. He wanted to turn away from the disgust that would shortly flow over her face. Only it didn't. Her expression remained calm and unreadable.

"Yes," he choked out.

"You have so much weight on your shoulders," she whispered, reaching up to stroke her hand over one of them.

"Much of which I put there myself," he said. "I did this."

"Not alone," she reminded him, her grip tightening on his arm. He stared at her, and for a moment just a tiny fraction of the weight that he carried lessened. He could breathe again.

But it couldn't last. "Either way, the result is the same."

She was very still, and then she slowly slid her hand away. His body mourned the loss. "I understand. I must confess to you that I don't like it."

"No?" he whispered.

She smiled, a sad and small expression that hit him in the stomach. "If my reaction to the kiss didn't spell it out to you, let me be clear. I *want*, too, Baldwin. I've been shocked by how deeply I felt connected to you, even after that first night. But I've known my position for a long time. I never assumed it would or even *could* be elevated. That wasn't my purpose in coming here. So it seems we must just be...*friends*."

Pain ripped through him at that kind offer. One he didn't deserve but meant so very much to him. "I would be honored to be your friend, Helena Monroe."

She stood and he followed her to her feet. She slid her hand through his elbow and smiled up at him. He could see the lie in that expression. The pain behind it. It mirrored his own, but what was there to do? Life was not fair.

He knew that very well.

"Then we shall be friends," she said, and motioned to the house. "It will be enough."

He nodded as he began to guide her back to the house and the party within. But with every step, he felt the weight of her fingers around his bicep. The warmth of her body beside him. He felt the relief that confession had given to him. Not just confession to anyone, but to *this* woman who had inspired his trust so easily.

And he knew being her friend was not enough. Could never be enough. But it was the only option.

CHAPTER NINE

"Do you have any news to report?"

Baldwin had been staring into his tea, stirring it aimlessly, but now his mother's voice broke into his fog and he jerked his head up to look at her. He found her watching him, concern in every line of her face.

"News?" he asked. "Regarding?"

"It's been a week since your sister's gathering," the duchess said, flexing her hands open and shut in a nervous display. "I know you've gone to a few parties since then and I haven't been to all of them. I was simply wondering if you'd enjoyed the company of any of our—our prospects?"

Baldwin paused before responding, for his mind was consumed with only one woman: Helena. Since Charlotte's party, since their passionate kiss in the garden, all there had been was her. And though he couldn't explain the full truth to his mother, that was a big part of why he couldn't concentrate on anyone or anything else.

"You know how the beginning of the Season is," he explained with a wave of his hand. "A crush, everyone circling. In a few weeks it will calm down and I'll be able to find more time to approach each lady individually."

His mother's lips pursed. "Baldwin, I do worry so."

Tension flooded him, pleasant thoughts of Helena fading into the background at last. "I know. I'm sorry. I do not have any intention of not doing as you wish."

"Of course you don't," the duchess said, reaching out to touch his arm. "I didn't mean to imply otherwise." She paced away, and for a moment Baldwin thought the conversation might be at its end. But then she turned back, determination lining her expression. "I think we ought to have a country party."

He leaned back. "A country party? Now?"

"Yes," she said. "A week would be enough time to let the servants out in Sheffield plan. It's only two-day ride for anyone we would invite in London."

"And you want to get these prospects alone," he said, folding his arms and spearing her with a hard glance.

She shook her head. "You needn't sound so ominous! They wouldn't be alone. We would invite others. To only invite the prospects would be too obvious. I would invite your married friends."

"Far less obvious, yes," he snorted.

She glared at him. "I hear told that the Earl of Grifford is back on the market after his wife's death. I could invite him. He's older and he won't interfere with your goals. And Matthew or Hugh or—well, not Robert. He'll just ruin all the young ladies he comes in contact with."

Baldwin stared in shock. She was not incorrect in her assessment of Robert, Duke of Roseford. Aside from being a loyal friend and an incredibly intelligent mind, he was also known as a rake of the highest order. Still, one didn't expect a lady to acknowledge that fact.

"You mean to invite gentlemen who you don't believe will intrude upon my various courtships," he said.

Her lips parted. "I know it all sounds mercenary and I don't like it any more than you do. Your sister married the love of her life—I'm not immune to the fact that life is demanding you not be allowed to do the same."

Once again, Baldwin flashed to images of Helena, her arms coming around him as she murmured out a deep sound of pleasure. He cleared his throat. "Most don't get as lucky as our

Charlotte," he said, trying to sound nonchalant.

"Well, at the very least I want you to see if you could *like* one of these women. That is a start." The duchess bent her head. "A country party solves our problems."

Baldwin could see that she was determined and that doing as she requested would take some amount of pressure off her shoulders. He owed her that. "Very well. Send word to Sheffield and mail your invitations to prospect and friend alike. A week in the country could do us all good."

She smiled, relief slashing across her face. "Excellent. I'll invite the prospects and the others we discussed."

Baldwin hesitated. "Including Miss Shephard?"

Her face fell a fraction. "I realize you've spent a bit more time with the Americans than with anyone else. Are you saying you don't like Charity at all?"

Baldwin swallowed. He hadn't really paid much attention to Helena's cousin. Fifty-thousand pounds or no, he could not fathom pursuing her and having Helena close by the entire time. It seemed an exercise in cruelty to them both.

"Have a mind, dear," the duchess said. "Her father is a bit overbearing, I know. In private, without him interfering and trying to manage any courtship she might have, she could be more...palatable."

Baldwin searched his mind, trying to find an argument against Charity. But the only one that screamed out at him was Helena. And he couldn't exactly explain that to his mother. She would be appalled that he had dragged a young lady he could have no true designs upon out to the garden and then kissed her. Yet another item on the list of his bad behaviors.

"Of course you shall invite them," he said with a sigh. "Though I would not get your hopes up that Charity will be my match."

She nodded. "I understand. Well, I will be off to write letters and make arrangements. I'll send you an accounting of everyone who says yes once it is finished." He moved to escort her back to the hall, and she leaned up to kiss his cheek as

Walker called for her carriage. "I know this is hard for you, dearest," she said softly. "But you're trying and that's all anyone can expect."

He smiled as her vehicle was brought round. "Good afternoon, Mama. Thank you again for all your help."

She left, and he watched as she was helped into her carriage. But as he waved her away, his mind kept returning to Helena Monroe. In truth, he would not be sorry to have a little time with her in the country. She was the only person in the world to know the full extent of his secret. Assuming she had not become disgusted with him the more she thought of what he'd done, it might be nice to have a friend who truly understood his position.

Although when he thought of her, lovely Helena, friendship was not what was on his mind. Which meant he'd have to change it. As quickly as possible.

Helena stared at her uneaten plate of supper and tried to force her mind to think of anything other than the topic that dominated it. Baldwin. He had been her only focus, her only thought, her only dream for seven long days. Since Charlotte's party. Since Baldwin's searing kiss and devastating confession.

"An invitation has arrived, sir," Aniston said as he entered the room, a folded envelope on a silver platter.

Her uncle glanced up and his eyes went wide at the seal on the front of the paper: an *S* with a riot of wheat around it. Helena gripped her fork tighter, for she had memorized that same seal and even drawn it out, in the secret pages of her journal.

Sheffield.

Uncle Peter rudely waved Aniston off and unfolded the paper with a sharp glance for Charity. "Here, girl, something to celebrate. I'll read it out loud. 'Your presence is requested at the country gathering of the Duke of Sheffield. Guests will gather for a week staring Sunday next.'" His eyes glittered. "And there's more, but that's the important part."

Charity slid her fork along her empty plate. "I don't know why I'd celebrate. The Duke of Sheffield showed no interest in me at his sister's party last week. And his friend Tyndale is quite handsome, but he seemed more enamored of *Helena*."

Helena jolted at the very unfair accusation. "I promise you, Charity, Tyndale was only being polite to me. He has no interest whatsoever."

Her uncle glared at her. "Charity is correct, though, that you did draw the attention of the Duke of Tyndale for far too long. We shall go, Charity, for Sheffield is too important to turn down, and who knows who else shall be there for you to exhibit to."

Helena's heart leapt. Go to Baldwin's country estate? A week in his company? The thought was both thrilling and heartbreaking after their last encounter. And yet she longed to see him. They had not been at any of the same events in the seven days since their kiss, and she wanted to reach out to him. To ask him if he regretted his confession to her in the garden. To find out if she could help him in any way, even if she could never have anything more than a friendship with him.

"Helena, you shall not attend," her uncle said, his harsh tone interrupting her thoughts.

She jerked her gaze to him in shock. "What? Uncle, you cannot mean that! I'm Charity's companion, this is why you brought—"

"Yes, but in the time we've been here you have only proven your own mother and father correct. You are becoming a liability, and I think you must be sent home before you ruin things for Charity as you ruined them for yourself."

Helena shoved her hands into her lap, praying that the hot tears that stung her eyes would not fall. Her uncle was so wrong about his accusations on her character, but it didn't matter. Nothing mattered except that he had decided she was unworthy and that was the end of it.

"Papa!" Charity said, shaking her head. "You cannot send Helena home."

Helena glanced at her in surprise. Charity, defending her? That would be something new.

"And why not?" Uncle Peter blustered.

Charity folded her arms. "Ladies of style and grace need a companion. How humiliating would it be for me to have to explain we sent mine home? You don't want me to look a fool do you? Helena will behave, especially now that she knows how serious you are."

Helena's cheeks burned, but she said nothing as Uncle Peter pondered Charity's words. Finally he nodded. "Paying a companion would be a waste of money at any rate. Fine, Helena, you shall stay and attend with us. But you will keep your mind focused on your duties. Is that clear?"

Helena pushed at the stubborn streak in her. The one that wanted to scream at her uncle about what had really happened to cause her fall. About her value as a person. But she couldn't do those things. Anything she said would fall on deaf ears anyway. He cared nothing for her.

She straightened her shoulders and swallowed her pride. "Of course. I…apologize for anything untoward you think I've done. My focus is entirely on Charity. I will behave as you expect me to do."

He nodded and then turned to Charity to talk about landing dukes. Helena settled back in her chair with a deep sigh. Her uncle and cousin had no idea exactly how right she had to make her mind if she were going into Baldwin's space.

It would be a challenge like no other. One she had to pass in order to survive.

CHAPTER TEN

There had never been a week that passed so slowly, especially the final two days, which Helena had spent in the carriage, listening to her uncle drone on endlessly. But now as the vehicle rolled up the long, winding lanes of Baldwin's estate, she couldn't help but thrill. She and Charity stared out the window together, her cousin commenting on the pretty trees that lined the lane.

But when the carriage turned, they both gasped, for there was Baldwin's estate house, rising up before them. Not just a house, though, a castle! With high stone walls and turrets to make it complete. It was everything out of Arthurian legends that had enthralled her as a child in America.

Whoever Baldwin married would be a princess, indeed, assuming she brought enough coin to keep the kingdom afloat.

"He must be rolling in blunt," Charity laughed.

Helena pursed her lips with displeasure. That was the vision Baldwin wished to put forth, of course—that his situation was safe and secure. She knew better.

"He won't even need your money, Papa," Charity continued with a giggle.

Uncle Peter grunted and his expression was dark and grumpy, as usual. "He'll take it, I'm sure. Now get ready, they're coming to open the doors."

Helena held back, trying to calm her racing heart, as

Baldwin's servants opened the doors and helped down Charity and her father. Of course, the two of them started up the stairs without waiting for her, making clear once more her position in the family. Helena sighed and smiled at the footman who assisted her. Finally, she allowed herself to look up at the landing on the house.

Baldwin was there, standing with his mother, Charlotte and the Duke of Donburrow. He was talking to her uncle and Charity, but he glanced down at her as she slowly mounted the stairs, and his dark eyes flowed over her until she felt warm from her head to her toes.

Seeing him was just as powerful as she feared it would be. It brought back all the feelings she'd been telling herself she could stifle. And all the memories of the trust he'd put in her and the pain she'd seen during his desperate confession.

She forced a smile in the hopes that it would ease any concerns he had about giving her his secrets. She would protect them well.

As her uncle and cousin stepped away to say hello to the duchess, Baldwin came down to meet her. "Hello," he said softly.

She smiled again, but this time it felt so very much weaker. It was impossible to be strong when he was standing *right there* and he was so damned beautiful.

"Your Grace," she said. "Your home is lovely."

He glanced up and she saw that flicker of trouble cross his expression. Only now she knew exactly why he feared. Why he hesitated. Why he frowned so often.

"Thank you, Helena," he replied at last. "I'm glad you could come."

"I'm glad to be here," she assured him.

She wanted to take his hand. Her own actually twitched like it would move of its own accord, and she had to fist it at her side to keep that from happening. He never moved, just stood looking at her. The moment stretched between them, just a bit too long, and she forced herself to step away.

"Helena!" Charlotte called out with a wide smile.

Helena glanced at Baldwin one last time, then moved toward her friend. She was surprised that Charlotte pulled her in for a hug and Ewan squeezed her hand gently as they chatted. But before she could get too involved with them, Uncle Peter barked, "Helena, come along. Your cousin needs your help!"

"I'm sorry, excuse me," she muttered with a blush, then scurried up the stairs to fall in step beside Charity. She didn't dare look back at either Charlotte or Baldwin. She feared they'd both be watching her. One with pity or even judgment. One with heat.

She could bear neither in that moment.

The servants took them to the top of the stairs and down the hall. Uncle Peter was taken to one room, while Charity and Helena were taken to another. As the butler drew the door open, Helena gasped. It was beautiful, with a view that looked over the expansive garden and a huge four-poster bed.

"Fit for a *queen*," Charity giggled as Walker excused himself and left them alone for a moment. She moved to the bed and flopped herself across the intricately stitched coverlet. "Or a duchess. This must be the nicest room in the house—I hope it means he likes me more than he's let on."

Helena shifted. It truly was a beautiful space. There were so many greens in the tasteful décor all around them. It was lovely and soothing.

"Or maybe it's *you* he likes."

Helena froze at the window, staring out into the garden. She swallowed hard, trying to make her expression serene as she looked back at her cousin at last. "I have no idea what you are talking about. The Duke of Sheffield like me?"

Charity folded her arms. "I haven't said anything, but I saw you two sneak out together from the Donburrow party last week."

Helena's lips parted. That no one had seemed to notice their brief absence had been the greatest of reliefs. She'd never known Charity to be discreet about anything, so she was shocked her cousin had kept that secret.

It could not bode well.

"Add that to when I found you alone in his home in London," Charity continued, ticking evidence of Helena's sins off on her fingers. "Then today when you came up the stairs and he met you? I saw some kind of...*connection* between you."

Helena's heart throbbed. The last thing she needed was for Charity to report whatever she believed to her father. He'd already threatened Helena once. She didn't need more of the same.

"I'm certain you're seeing things. The man is polite, that is all." Helena's tone was breathless even though she didn't want it to be.

Her cousin moved on her, bright eyes flashing with annoyance. "As Papa said so many times, you're here for *me*. I defended you before, but I won't do it again if you insist on putting yourself where you don't belong."

Helena swallowed. "Of course."

Charity bobbed her head with another glare. "I see there's a connecting room here. It's likely to my sitting room. If there is a settee there, you can sleep on it. I don't feel like sharing the big bed. Now I intend to take a nap until my things arrive and then you can help me pick my clothes for the supper tonight."

Helena sighed and backed from the room into the connecting sitting room. "Very well."

She shut the door and stuck out her tongue at it the way she wished she could do to her cousin's face. But she couldn't. She stomped to the settee that would apparently be her bed and flopped down on it. At least it was comfortable and it was angled so she could see out the floor-to-ceiling window that overlooked another fine view of Baldwin's gardens.

Her mind turned as she lay there looking at that wonderful sea of green. In a way, Charity was right. Helena had no right to connect with a duke who had made it clear he could not pursue her, even if they both felt the connection between them.

But that didn't mean the connection melted away. She'd felt

it in Baldwin's stare, in the way he'd come to her on the stairs. In the way her body had responded to him even when she didn't want it to do so.

And it also didn't mean that she didn't still feel a driving desire to offer him support. Thanks to how jealously he'd guarded his secrets from everyone else in his life, she was likely the only one he could turn to.

So despite her cousin's warnings and her uncle's bluster, she knew that at some point during this weeklong gathering, she was going to reach out to Baldwin. As a friend and a confidante.

And there was nothing they could do to stop her.

All Baldwin had to do was stay away from Helena. He'd been reminding himself of that fact since their awkward exchange on the landing, when he'd very nearly caught her in his arms and kissed her until she couldn't breathe. That moment of sharp desire had been a reminder that he couldn't control himself.

So avoidance was the key.

Except now, as he stood in his ballroom, surrounded by spinning couples and longtime friends, his vow seemed impossible to keep. Helena was everywhere. When he looked into the crowd, he found her standing with her cousin. Or worse, with his friends, where she laughed and smiled and looked like she fit perfectly.

When he turned to speak to a servant, there she was, collecting drinks for her horrible family, who treated her like she was less than a lady.

When he walked through the crowd, he had to dodge her, stepping out of his way to stay out of hers.

She was everywhere, both physically and in his addled mind, and there seemed to be nothing he could do to lessen the pulsing desire he felt for her. Even as he danced with each and every prospect his mother had brought here for him, the only thing he thought about when they were in his arms was that not a one of them was Helena Monroe.

"I think Charity Shephard is next."

He jumped, for he had not realized his mother had approached him as he stood, staring off toward Helena and brooding about the lack of fairness in this bloody situation.

"Charity?" he repeated as he glanced at the duchess.

She tilted her head in confusion. "You've danced with all the rest. Charity is the last of the prospects."

His stomach turned. Not only did he not particularly *like* Charity Shephard after watching how she treated Helena, but the idea of pursuing her was the worst thing he had ever pondered. What would he do, marry Charity and have Helena come into his home as her companion? Spend his life in the arms of one woman while the one he really wanted traipsed through his halls being…her?

Fifty thousand pounds would create more problems than it solved at that point.

But there was no saying that to his mother, so he bobbed his head. "Of course. It looks like she's just finishing a turn with the Earl of Grifford at present. Once they have finished, I will see if her dance card is open for the next."

She reached out to catch his arm as he began to walk away, and he turned his attention back to her. "You are pale," she said softly. "Is everything well? Did you like *any* of the young ladies?"

He almost laughed, but he bit it back and tried to put a serene expression on his face. "Certainly they are all lovely ladies."

Her expression pinched, like she didn't like that vague praise, but she released him so he could go to the last on his hated list.

The song ended, and Charity and her partner left the floor together. He watched as the earl bowed over her hand. To his surprise, she actually tittered as she said farewell to him. But at last she was left standing alone. He was grateful to have caught her between dances. Her father was even worse than she was, a blustering fool who thought his money gave him class when it certainly did not. Baldwin had no desire to talk to him.

She smiled as he approached, and there was a moment when he could admit she was lovely. She had blonde hair and bright blue eyes. Her gown was perfection, not too revealing but still alluring.

Yes, she would make a pretty piece on any man's arm. And with her fortune to boot, a hundred mercenaries would soon be knocking at her door.

Baldwin hated that he had to be one of them.

"Good evening, Miss Shephard," he said with a stiff bow as he reached her side.

"Your Grace," she said with a coy smile. There was nothing real about it—it was all put on for a show. Unlike Helena, who was only real. "I wondered when you would seek me out."

He blinked at the playful forwardness of her words. "Did you?"

"I saw that you have danced with all the eligible young ladies in the room."

He frowned. Well, he could add *observant* to this young woman's list of qualities, such as they were. Something he'd have to be aware of.

"I have saved the best for last, it seems," he said, and hated how untrue the words sounded. But Charity liked them, for she blushed. "Is the next song open on your dance card?"

She nodded, and took his arm to allow him to lead her to their places. He stared at her as they waited and others took the floor. He could think of nothing to say to this woman. Nothing he wanted to know.

It was beastly of him, of course, not to give a damn. But how could he dare when he knew what would happen if Charity became the focused object of his pursuit?

The music swelled and he let out a soft breath. A damned waltz. Of course it was. She stepped up into his embrace and they began to turn around the floor in what felt far too close proximity.

"Your home is lovely," she said, pulling him from his thoughts and reminding him once again how rude he was being.

"Thank you," he said.

"I can't imagine you prefer it to London, though," she continued.

He shrugged. "They both have their advantages."

She laughed. "Do they? London is so exciting. There is always some adventure to be had there, some new shop to find or thing to see."

"I suppose," he said. Honestly, he had not thought of London in that way in a very long time. It was a place where creditors could show up on one's doors without warning and make a scene that would someday bring everything down around him.

"My father has always been obsessed with this country," she continued. "He liked your side better in the revolution, though he never talks about it much at home, for obvious reasons."

"Yes, I assume that would have him counted as a traitor," Baldwin drawled.

She didn't seem to take offense. "Oh, yes, he must keep his sentiments to himself. Whisper them to others who think as he does while he plays patriot in public so that he can continue to draw in funds."

Baldwin's stomach turned at such duplicity. But then, he was hardly better. All that he was doing was false, meant to keep his family afloat.

Charity was oblivious to his feelings and continued, "When he said he was bringing us here for a Season, I was hesitant, but I suppose I'm glad now. It got Helena and me out of boring old Boston!"

Baldwin glanced down at her. He had not wanted to dance with her, but now he saw a unique opportunity in doing so. He could ask her questions and find out more about Helena.

"It must be helpful to have a companion in your travels," he suggested carefully.

"I suppose," she said, wrinkling her nose. "Although Helena was not much of a companion on the trip. She spent most of the crossing casting up her accounts on the prow of the boat."

Baldwin stifled a smile at that tidbit. Though he didn't like to hear of her suffering, he could file that information away about her. No boats.

"And do you two share the same…interests?" he said, still treading very carefully.

"Hardly," Charity laughed. "Helena is a bookworm. You should see her devour them, one after another. She'd read the instructions on a tonic bottle and be enthralled. I prefer excitement. My papa owns a racehorse and he's taken me dozens of times. I've even won some coin at it."

She said the last with a little wink and his stomach turned. One more reason to avoid Charity as a bride. The last thing his family needed was another gambler. He'd had quite enough excitement in his day—he didn't need her dragging him out and insisting she spend their money on horses.

"Some have the luck," he said as he turned her around the floor once more. When would this song end? It felt like it had been going on forever. "Did you and Miss Monroe grow up together?"

Charity's eyes narrowed. "You are very interested in my cousin."

Baldwin drew back. Damn, he'd pushed too far. Now he had to back himself down without rousing more of her suspicion. "Not at all," he lied. "I'm interested in you, of course, as we are dancing. I only inquired after your childhood."

She didn't look convinced, but launched into a recitation of her days in Boston as a girl. She never once mentioned Helena, and Baldwin found himself drifting into his own thoughts, counting the steps and the beats to the dance as he waited for it to just end.

And at last, it did. He smiled in relief at Charity as he guided her from the floor and toward her father. "Thank you again for the dance, Miss Shephard."

She eyed him closely as he brought her to her father. "And to you, Your Grace. Perhaps when next we speak, we can talk of more interesting things than my cousin."

He pinched his lips at her pointed tone, nodded to her father and left her side. It was like he was being freed from prison, and he drew a long breath. Now he had fulfilled his duty, at least for tonight. He'd danced with the prospects, appeased his mother and made a few mental notes here and there about them.

So he was free to do as he pleased. He glanced around the room and found Helena standing along the wall. She was alone, with a wistful expression that could not be denied, watching the couples who had retaken the floor as they waited for the next song to begin. She wanted to dance. And he wanted desperately to dance with her.

In that moment, he knew he would. She would be his reward for enduring the evening so far. What could be the harm?

He took a step toward her, but before he could cross the room, Walker rushed up to his side. "Your Grace?"

He turned toward his butler with a groan. "Yes, Walker, what is it?"

"I'm sorry to disturb in the midst of the party, but you have a message."

"Can it not wait?"

Walker shook his head. "I don't think so, sir. It is from Mr. Deacon."

Baldwin froze. Deacon was the man he'd hired to investigate the missing debts owed by the estate. "When did it arrive?"

"Just now, Your Grace," Walker said. "And since you'd told me before that any correspondence from the man was—"

"Urgent, yes," he said. "It is. I assume you deposited the message in my study?"

Walker nodded and Baldwin sighed as he cast one more glance over his shoulder toward Helena. She was still alone, but now she was looking at him from across the room. He shivered under her focused stare and longed to cross to her, to gather her up and forget the troubles that weighed so heavily upon him.

But it seemed his moment with her was not to be. At least not now. Not there.

CHAPTER ELEVEN

Helena watched Baldwin leave the ballroom, and her heart sank. His *expression*. Oh, it was awful. Like a man being led to the gallows. It wasn't as if he'd looked pleased during the rest of the night. She'd seen the tension on his face as he interacted with his guests, but this was something different.

Something dreadful.

She longed to go to him, to offer him the friendship they had both vowed was all they could share. She was a fool.

"Helena."

She turned and smiled as Adelaide, Duchess of Northfield, slid up beside her and gave her a little squeeze.

"Adelaide, oh, you look beautiful!"

And she did. The duchess was the epitome of sophistication in a gold-and-silver gown with intricate braiding and a flowing skirt that swirled when she turned. Unlike the other ladies in the room, whose hair was pulled high to accentuate cheekbones and necks, her companion's blonde locks were done looser and framed her pretty face to perfection.

"Thank you," Adelaide said with a little blush. "It is still odd for me to come out into Society with such…fanfare."

Helena wrinkled her brow. "You didn't before?"

"Oh no," Adelaide laughed. "I stood along the wall for many years. It is Graham who convinces me to be…" The duchess looked across the room to where Graham was standing, laughing heartily with Simon. "…more."

Helena shifted, for there was no denying the love this woman felt for her husband. Actually, that was the common thread that seemed to tangle in all the members of the duke club who had married. They all loved deeply, passionately, truly.

It was truly something to behold.

"I have a hard time imagining you as a wallflower," Helena said with a laugh. "You are so confident and lovely."

"Love helps with that," Adelaide said, tearing her gaze away from the husband. "And practice. The more I dance and, as Graham calls it, *exhibit*, the easier it gets."

Helena shook her head. "I used to like to dance. Not exhibit, but dancing was one of my favorite pastimes before—"

She cut herself off. Had she truly been on the cusp of telling this lady, this stranger, about her past? A faux pas of the highest order. Her uncle would be enraged, despite the fact that he always liked to imply she was a scandal in the flesh. But to tell the particulars was something different. Not to mention if she did, the story would spread through their tight little circle, and then what would happen?

Her lovely new friendships would dissolve as swiftly as her ones in Boston had.

Adelaide examined her a bit closer, but she did not press. "If you like to dance, I'm surprised you have not done it. Baldwin seemed to be taking a turn with all the unmarried ladies, though I do not see him here at present."

Helena swallowed. "Sheffield was dancing with the *eligible* ladies."

"You are not eligible? Are you married and we did not know it?"

"No." Helena shook her head. "You are all lovely to pretend that I'm in the same sphere as you are, but it isn't true. I'm not eligible because I'm here as a companion. Even if I weren't I am certainly out of Baldwin—er, Sheffield's league."

Adelaide shrugged. "Emma felt the same way about James. Certainly I did with Graham. You would be surprised how little you know about men and what they want in their hearts. I think they are often surprised when it runs them over like an out-of-control phaeton. At least that is how Graham describes his feelings for me. Romantic, though a bit violent, I keep telling him."

Helena stared. "I have seen Emma with Abernathe. They are so deeply in love. And right now your husband is staring at you like you are a chocolate and he's a starving man."

Adelaide glanced over her shoulder again, and she shivered ever so slightly as she noticed the look on Graham's face. "The love you see now does not change the circumstances of our beginnings. I'm just saying, don't count yourself out when it comes to Baldwin."

"It's different with me," Helena whispered, and ducked her head. "With us."

Adelaide lifted a hand and covered her smile briefly. When Helena's lips parted, she shook her head. "I know I'm laughing, but it isn't *at* you. It's just that I bet Meg a pound that you'd say just that. So she owes me and I thank you, for I'll shamelessly hold it over her head."

Helena forced a smile. She saw the humor, but Adelaide didn't know the circumstances. The barriers that could never, ever be crossed.

"Chances at happiness come so rarely, Helena," Adelaide said, gentler now as she took both Helena's hands. "Don't discount even their possibility, or there will be nothing worth looking forward to."

Helena sighed, and her mind filled for a brief moment with those possibilities. With more kisses in gardens. With that connection that had been instantaneous and so powerful that it had set her on her heels in surprise.

"I suppose you are right," she found herself whispering. "I appreciate the support anyway."

"It's yours," Adelaide said. "From all of us." She grinned. "Now here comes my lovely husband and Simon."

Helena wiped her emotions away and smiled as the men

joined them. Graham immediately reached out and settled his hand into the small of Adelaide's back. Their love was palpable in that moment, and Helena was even more jealous of her new friend's obvious happiness.

"Helena was just telling me how much she likes to dance," Adelaide said.

"Ah," Simon said with a smile for her. "Well, I am the best dancer in our group."

"And the most modest," Graham said with a laugh.

"You shouldn't talk the way you lumber," Simon said with a roll of his eyes in Helena's direction.

"I take offense to that—my husband has never lumbered in his life," Adelaide said.

Helena wondered at it all. They were all so playful and funny, and they included her so effortlessly. And it was bewitching to pretend she could belong with them. Now or in the future.

Simon shook his head. "Ignore them, they are simply jealous of my skills. I would be delighted to share the next with you, unless you have another partner in mind."

Helena glanced to the door where Baldwin had left the ballroom moments before. Then she smiled at Simon. "I would be honored, Your Grace, as long as Meg wouldn't mind."

"Oh, she wouldn't," he said as he offered her an arm and led her to the dancefloor. But as they began the intricate steps of the jig the orchestra played next, Helena couldn't help but think once more of Baldwin's face when he left the ballroom.

And wish that she could find a way to help him. Even though that wasn't her place.

Baldwin stared at the letter that had been left on his desk for what had to be the tenth time in a half hour. The words swam, just as they had from the first moment he read them. Now he could hardly see them, but it didn't matter.

They were seared onto his soul, statements he would never forget even if he tried with all his might.

"'The missing debts have been found,'" he said out loud, flinching as his hands began to shake. "'Or their previous whereabouts were discovered, held by three gentlemen.'"

He swallowed as he got up and tossed the letter aside. He'd been waiting to hear this, to know who held his fate in their hands, who could drop the guillotine on his neck.

Only the men who had owned those debts no longer did. They'd sold them, all on the same day, all through the same solicitor.

Which meant that one man probably held them now. Someone who had discovered and purchased the debts in a calculated way and protected his identity through the solicitor, who refused to give Baldwin's man any further information, including terms of repayment.

It turned his stomach to think of what the intentions of such a man might be. To think of the nightmares he could create with a flick of his wrist.

Baldwin paced to the sideboard and pulled out a bottle of scotch. He didn't bother with a glass, but slung himself into the seat before the fire and took a long swig. He should go back to his party, but right now he couldn't even think of roaming around amongst prospects and friends, pretending to be well when his head was spinning and his heart hurting.

Right now he wanted to forget. And this was the best way he knew how.

Helena crept up the quiet hallway, her skirt fisted in her hand as she looked from one closed door to the next, trying to find some hint as to where she should go.

It had been hours since Baldwin's departure from the

ballroom, his face pinched and pained. She'd waited for him to come back, trying to pretend like his whereabouts meant nothing to her. It became harder and harder as the whispers started. The questions as to why their host had abandoned the party so abruptly.

She'd seen the worry on Charlotte's face and on the Duchess of Sheffield's as they made excuses and exchanged looks. With every moment, Helena's desire to help Baldwin grew. And now, with the party winding to a close and her cousin returning to their room to be helped to bed by her maid, Helena knew this was her only chance to do so.

She turned another corner in the endless hallway and stopped. While most of the rooms were dark, there was a small sliver of light coming from under one door at the end of this hall. Her heart began to pound as she moved toward it, hoping she'd found Baldwin. Fearful she had. Totally lost as to what she'd do if he was behind that door.

She knocked, but there was no answer. Her shoulders slumped. The room was likely empty. She moved to go, but before she could step away there was the clatter of something hitting the ground and a muffled curse from behind the door.

She reached out and pushed the door open.

If there had been a lamp lighting the room, it had long since burned out. The fire was all that remained, and it flickered and sent long shadows throughout the chamber. It was a study, much like the one in Baldwin's London home.

When she turned to look at the fire, there he was. He had been seated in front of the mantel, but now he rose, rather awkwardly and stared at her.

He gripped a bottle in his hand. A half-empty bottle, at that. His jacket was gone, his cravat was gone and his shirt was half undone, revealing a shocking expanse of skin peppered with wiry chest hair that a lady should not see. Not when she had such wicked thoughts about a gentleman, at any rate.

She caught her breath and stared at him. He stared right back, unblinking, unmoving, unreadable.

"Are you a dream?" he finally asked, his words just ever so slightly slurred.

She glanced over her shoulder. He would not want others to find him this way. She stepped into the room and pulled it shut behind her. For a moment she hesitated, and then she turned the key in the lock, granting them privacy and a heavy dose of inappropriate aloneness.

"No," she whispered when she could find her voice.

"That's worse, actually," he muttered, and collapsed back into the chair with a grunt. The bottle in his fingers slid free and rolled away, spilling the remainder of its contents on the carpet. "If you were a dream, I could have what I want."

She moved forward, confused and driven and attracted and terrified all at once. "You left your party, Baldwin," she said gently. "I was worried when you didn't return."

"Everyone else gets what they want," he said, ignoring what she was saying. "Have you ever noticed that?"

She eased into the chair beside his and leaned forward, examining his face carefully. She'd thought him unreadable, but that was wrong. No, emotions were there. There were just so many that it was hard to parse them all out.

"Some people are lucky," she conceded.

He laughed, but there was no pleasure in the sound. No light. No happiness. It was harsh and cold. "Oh yes, so many. My friends are *lucky*. Half of them are married and oh-so happy."

She frowned. "You cannot mean that you'd begrudge them that, Baldwin. I know you care for them."

The hardness of his face softened a little, and he shrugged. "No, not begrudge. They earned it. They deserve their joy. But I still have to look at it, don't I? Those little looks between them, their endless comments about how I should marry for love. 'Marry for *love*, Baldwin.' They have no idea."

She swallowed hard. "No, they don't. You haven't told them the truth."

He stared at her, and it was like he saw her for the first time all over again. "You're going to be very rational, aren't you?"

She smiled despite the precarious situation. "I suppose I am."

"Why?" he asked. "It's not like you get what you want, either. Here we are, two people who'll *never* get what they want because of what someone else did. Because of what we did to ourselves."

She flinched. He had no idea what he was saying, but he was awfully close to home, to her secrets that she had to keep silent in order to find any kind of peace with her past. She bent her head.

"I suppose there is such a thing as acceptance, Baldwin. Torturing myself does no good."

"Yes, I'm torturing myself," he agreed. To her surprise, he suddenly leaned forward, nearly off the chair. His face was very close now, too close. "You're here, aren't you? You're here under my roof. In a bed just ten or twelve doors from my own. In my study with the door locked. You are a torture, Helena Monroe. Because what I want, more than anything in the world right now…is *you*."

The slurring had gone out of his words as he said them. Like what he said was true enough that it overcame tipsy foolishness. She stared at him, at that handsome face so close to her own. Every rational thing in her screamed at her to get up and walk away. To pretend like this had never happened.

Except rationality wasn't her most powerful drive in that moment. So instead of listening to that very wise voice, she reached out and let her hand cup his cheek.

He let out a long, steady hiss of breath. He caught the edge of her chair and dragged it forward, the legs screeching against the floor as he pulled her into the space between his legs. She was shaking as she drew her fingers up through his hair.

He grunted out some incoherent sound, and then he leaned in and his mouth touched hers.

In the garden, his kiss had been gentle. Tentative, even. The kiss of a man with all his senses and reason. This was something entirely different. The alcohol had not stolen his senses, but dulled them a little and left him much wilder. His lips slanted over hers, hard and demanding, and she opened without hesitation. He drove in, tangling his tongue with hers. She tasted scotch and desperation and drive and need. She found herself lifting closer, drowning in his kiss.

He pulled her, and she tumbled off her chair and firmly into his lap. His fingers pushed into her hair, drawing down some of the locks as he kissed her and kissed her and kissed her.

She let him. He had been right that she would never have what she wanted. And yes, she had been telling him the truth when she said she accepted that fact. But there was also pain. And grief. But when he touched her all that faded away, and all that was left was the pulsing drive she felt to surrender to him.

His hands drifted lower as he kissed her, his fingers tracing her neck, her collarbone, the edge of her plain gown. Then they folded around her breast and she tilted her head back with a moan of pleasure. She hadn't expected that sensation, but there it was, powerful and wonderful and overwhelming all at once.

He lifted his mouth to her exposed throat and began to swirl little patterns with the tip of his tongue. She found herself rocking against him almost against her will, her fingertips digging into his chest as he did things to her that made her forget every other thing in the world but him.

His hand dragged from her breast and she was faintly aware through the fog of desire that it was drifting lower. He cupped her hip, then she felt her skirt hitching up. Up and up until the warm air that stirred from the fire tickled her calves and her knees.

Desire was like the ocean and she swam through it, knowing she had to surface, to become aware of her surroundings again. Somehow she managed to do so and stared down first at her uncovered legs and then at him.

"I-I don't—" she stammered, placing her hands on his to keep him from lifting her skirts all the more.

"I want to touch you," he explained, his voice very low and

soft and gentle. "Just touch you, Helena. Just give you pleasure because I want to see it. I want to feel it. But I'll stop if you give the word."

She could hardly breathe. It wasn't that she hadn't been in this position before. Oh, she had, but not like this. Not when it had been a pleasure rather than a terror. Not with a man she wanted. So she was tangled between harsh, horrible memories and an unexpected longing.

She shut her eyes. If her life was to be lived with an implied scandal trailing her wherever she went, if it was to be chasing after Charity and trying to avoid the wrath of her uncle, if it was to be acceptance...then being here with Baldwin, this was her last chance at having something just for herself. Something she longed for.

Something to erase the painful memories of the past. Or at least soften them slightly. With this man, she had no doubt she would be taken care of. Even a drink or two into his cups he didn't force or push or demand. He was *asking* for her leave.

And in that moment, she found herself nodding as she pulled her hand away.

"Y-yes," she choked out as she turned her face. "Yes."

CHAPTER TWELVE

"Someone hurt you," Baldwin said.

Helena stiffened at the words. They were a statement, not a question. Something he could see even with his drink-addled mind. She didn't look at him, but nodded.

For a moment he was still, and then she felt his finger touch her chin. He tugged and she was forced to look at him. He blinked a few times, like he was trying to clear his mind.

"Do you want this?" he repeated.

She swallowed. "I don't know," she admitted. "When you touch me…it makes me forget those other things. But I don't really know what you'll do or what I'll feel."

His brow wrinkled and his face softened. "Pleasure," he promised as he brushed his lips over hers again.

She sank into the kiss once more, loving how his tongue felt when it tangled with her own. It was heaven, it was heat, it was desire and pleasure. And somehow he was promising her more. She wanted more.

So when his hand tugged on her skirt again, she didn't stop him. She just continued kissing him in the hopes that her fears would stop flaring and she could just enjoy this stolen, wicked moment that he offered.

He bunched her skirt at her hips and then pressed a hand on her now-exposed knee. Through her stockings, she felt the heat of his palm as he squeezed gently. Then his fingers glided upward, slowly, tracing the line of her legs.

She shivered, for she'd never realized just how sensitive her legs were. But it was like being jolted awake when he touched her like this.

His kiss deepened as he slid that same hand from the front of her thigh to the inside. Her legs fell open of their own accord, even as she sucked in a breath of surprise and fear.

He pulled away from the kiss and stared into her eyes. "No matter how far I go, no matter what, you can tell me no."

She jerked out a nod as she looked down at the image of his hand on her leg. It looked so big there, so dark against the pale skin above her stocking, and it felt as warm as fire.

He held her gaze as he glided his fingers up higher, to the slit in her drawers. Gently he parted the fabric, and then his fingers wedged their way inside.

When he touched her sex, she jolted and he stopped moving, but just rested his palm there, flat and warm against her sensitive skin.

He leaned back in and his mouth found hers again. She was focused on his hand against her, that wicked hand covering the most private part of her. But as the kiss deepened once more, her focus softened, the fear lost its edge and she wrapped her arms around his neck with a sigh.

Only then did he begin to move his fingers again. He stroked along the outside of her folds, tracing her sex gently. Now that the shock had faded a fraction, the touch of his skin no longer felt so very frightening and foreign. It was nice, actually. Intimate. Warm.

Enticing.

He gently opened her, and she drew back with another gasp. "Stop?" he asked, his gaze fully focused on her face.

She shook her head. "No, I-I was just surprised."

"It won't hurt," he assured her. "I'm not going to penetrate. I just want to do…this…"

He began to swirl two fingers against her, gently at first, in some wonderful place she had never imagined existed in her body before. When he did, pleasure bolted through her, racing through her veins and her nerves and her skin and everything else. It was pleasure from every part in her body, and she shuddered as he increased the pressure ever so slightly.

"Baldwin," she croaked out.

He nodded and pressed his lips to her neck as he continued to circle, circle. She felt how wet she was from that touch, and yet that wetness made the electric current of desire all the stronger. It built and built, blossoming like a flower as he expertly pleasured her with nothing but his two fingers.

She found herself lifting into him, meeting the stroke of his hand halfway as her breath came short and her legs started to shake. This was…wonderful, different than anything she'd ever felt before.

But it was arcing out of control. And that terrified her and exhilarated her all at once. She might have asked him about it. She might have pulled away from the intensity, but at that moment the sensations crested and suddenly she was falling, falling over an edge of something she'd never known. Her body quaked in long waves of pleasure that rocked her every fiber. She clung to him, moaning out his name as her back arched and her feet flexed in her slippers.

At last the crisis faded and she went weak against his chest. He held her there as her breathing returned to normal and her vision cleared. She had no idea how long, for everything in her world felt very slow and sweet and focused on the trembling warmth that remained between her legs.

But at last she sat up slightly and blushed as she realized her position, still curled up on his lap. She made a move to go back to her own chair, but he caught her hand and drew her down to kiss her once more.

"Don't blush," he said. "That was wonderful."

She swallowed hard and nodded. "Yes. Wonderful."

He moved to stand, but when he did he staggered ever so slightly, catching himself on the arm of the chair where he'd just done such wicked things to her. She jolted and moved to catch his arm, helping him balance as he blinked in surprise.

"I hardly ever drink," he muttered. "Apparently I have little head for it anymore."

She couldn't help but smile. Leave it to Baldwin to remain in control even when he was in his cups. Enough control to pleasure her, and yet he hadn't asked her for anything in return. Even though she could see the harsh outline of his body against his trousers in the faint firelight.

"Do you need help upstairs to bed?" she asked.

His gaze jerked to her, and there was fire in it. Desire that hadn't faded even a fraction. Her body warmed at the sight of it, still tingling despite her needs being slaked.

"I can make it on my—" He released the chair and took a step, but staggered once more. He let out a long, ragged sigh. "Very well. I suppose I could use the help. There are back stairs that will help us hide from prying eyes."

She shook her head as she moved to his side. He hesitated, then slung an arm around her shoulder and leaned on her for support. The feel of him along the length of her body made everything seem very hot and close.

"It's late," she said, trying to keep her tone light. "I doubt we'll encounter anyone, back stairs or front. The party was wrapping up before I came to find you."

He let out a long sigh. "My mother and Charlotte will be upset I missed the remainder of the gathering. Seems I can do nothing right of late."

They exited into the hallway and she glanced at him from the corner of her eye. His mouth was set in a thin line and his gaze was straight ahead and filled with remorse. She couldn't help but reflect on how very lonely he must be. No one knew his secret—well, no one but her. So he was forced to pretend for the world.

She understood that better than most. She understood the lack of respite mistakes created.

She cleared her throat. "Do you want to tell me what happened that put you in this state?"

He was quiet for a moment, and then he grunted. "Drunk and ready to accost innocent ladies?"

She pursed her lips. How little he knew. "You are not *exactly* drunk and I do not feel accosted, Your Grace. So unless there were other ladies who called on you in your study tonight, please put that thought out of your mind." She shook her head. "I meant, what made you leave your party? And drink in the dark?"

"I thought women liked broody men," he said. "James, Graham…Robert…brooders all."

She glanced at him. "You don't have to tell me, of course."

They had reached the back stairs, and he gripped the banister as they made their way up slowly. "It's nothing," he mumbled.

She nodded slowly, trying to ignore the disappointment that rose up in her. His rejection reminded her of her place, the one they'd both forgotten when he confessed to her initially. Or when he'd touched her moments before.

"I understand," she said.

He waved his hand toward the door at the end of the hallway. "You don't," he said.

"I only want to help," she said.

He paused for a moment, then looked down at her. "You did. Tonight you did, for when I touched you I forgot every other thing." He leaned in to kiss her, then weaved.

"It's starting to catch up with you now, isn't it?" she asked, unable to stop the chuckle that escaped her lips.

"Apparently," he said with a laugh of his own.

She reached out and opened his chamber and together they moved inside.

"Come on then," she said, urging him through the sitting room and into the master chamber. She edged him forward. "To bed with you."

He staggered and flopped face-first onto the mattress. She lifted his feet up and began to work on his boots. It was a mighty feat, but she managed to loosen first one, then the other, and tug them both off. He sighed as she did so. "Thank you. I much prefer you to my regular valet."

She smiled, rather enamored with this silly man who now inhabited the usually serious body of the Duke of Sheffield. "Go to sleep now. It will be better in the morning."

He rolled to his side to face her. "It won't be. How I wish you could join me. That would make my morning better."

Her heart jumped. The suggestion was tempting, for certain. The idea of curling herself around this man in his bed. Of waking up to him beside her. Of waking up to more of that wonderful pleasure he had provided less than half an hour before.

She shook her head. "You know I can't," she whispered.

He didn't speak, but reached his hand out to awkwardly touch her face with his fingertips. Then he smiled and said, "Good night, lovely Helena."

"Good night," she said. She moved to extinguish the lamp, and as she did she heard the soft sound of a snore from the bed. She turned to examine him in firelight for the second time that night and found him already asleep. She leaned a little closer, indulging herself as she would likely never be allowed to do again.

He was so beautiful. Just perfectly formed in every way, and in his sleep the seriousness and worry was all gone from his face.

She leaned in and gently kissed his cheek. "Good night," she said again, and turned to leave the room.

But first she looked around. Unlike the rest of the house, which was still opulent, here she saw the effects of the financial struggles Baldwin faced. Everything was plain, from the worn furniture to the discolorations in the walls where pictures had clearly once hung but had now been removed, likely sold.

It was sobering, and she frowned as she slipped from the room and closed the door behind herself. She crept away hurriedly so she wouldn't be caught in such a terrible position, but as she moved toward the guest wing of the house, she couldn't help but ponder everything that had happened tonight, from the ball to the pleasure to the end.

She wanted to help Baldwin, but tonight he had helped her, without even meaning to. Without even trying. And she knew that she would never be the same.

CHAPTER THIRTEEN

Baldwin lifted his head with a moan. Pain shot through his entire skull and down his neck. He flopped back down face-first into his pillow and stayed there, blessedly surrounded by the darkness.

It had been a very long time since he drank to excess. A very, very long time since he had more than one glass of scotch out of politeness. Not that he hadn't earned that pleasure...or punishment, for it felt like a punishment now.

But his sense of responsibility always stopped him.

He rolled over slowly and grunted in pain once more. Everything was coming back to him now. The letter about the outstanding debts that could very well seal his fate. The decision to go drink that pain away.

And then Helena had come and—

He jerked to a seated position as he was overwhelmed with memories. Kissing her. Touching her...oh God, touching her.

There was a knock on his chamber door and he ignored it as he set his head in his hands. What had he done? They'd talked and he'd touched and then—then she'd told him that someone...hurt her. Rage swelled up in him at that thought. Rage at that faceless person. Rage at himself because despite her confession, he had continued on anyway. He had lifted her skirts and touched her. An ungentlemanly act that he wouldn't have done if he weren't tipsy.

The knock came again and he staggered from his bed. "What?"

It opened, but it wasn't a servant who peeked his head into the darkened chamber. It was Simon. Baldwin groaned.

"What do you want, Crestwood?" he mumbled as he relived last night over and over again, tormenting himself with both the pleasure of what he'd done and the incredible imprudence of it.

Simon strode through his sitting room and into his chamber. "We're riding, don't you remember? Were you still abed? I don't think I've ever known you to lollygag around after seven in your entire life."

Before Baldwin could retort, Simon went to the window and threw the curtains wide, sending a stream of bright sunshine cascading into the room. Baldwin flinched away from it, from the pain it brought. Pain he deserved, it seemed.

Simon stared at him, and the jovial, teasing smile that had been on his face faded slowly. "What is wrong with you? You look like hell."

Baldwin covered his face. He had kept so many lies from his best friends, his brothers, his family. Right now he had no ability to do so.

"I did something," he moaned as he dared to look at Simon again.

Simon moved on him, catching his arm gently. "What, what did you do?"

Baldwin turned away, questioning his decision to speak. But then, this was Simon. Simon had pursued his wife, Meg, despite the fact that she'd been engaged to Graham at the time. They had been imprudent with their passions, they'd nearly destroyed themselves and the entire group they called friends.

Simon, of all people, would understand him.

"I was half-drunk," he said. "It's no excuse. It was wrong."

Simon leaned in. "Baldwin, you are nothing but good and decent. Whatever you did, I'm certain it isn't as bad as you believe."

Baldwin tilted his head back, trying to find air. "Helena,"

he whispered at last. "She found me in that...state. She found me and I...I went too far."

Simon stared at him for a moment, then his eyes widened. "Are you telling me you took Helena Monroe to bed?"

"No," he said, lurching backward. Oh, that's what he'd wanted to do. Still wanted to do. But he couldn't. He couldn't no matter how much he wanted to. "No, but I...I touched her. In an ungentlemanly way."

Simon shook his head. "Baldwin, I've known you since you were twelve. You would never do something against a lady's will. It's clear that Helena is attracted to you, that you are attracted to her and despite everything, sometimes these things happen."

"That doesn't mean what I did was right. Even though she said yes, I...I can't pursue her."

Simon frowned. "Why?"

Baldwin caught his breath. "I can't, that's all. I don't want to get into it. I must find her, talk to her."

He moved to the boots that had been left neatly at the foot of his bed. He paused to stare at them. Helena had put them there. Helena had smiled at him, and he thought he vaguely remembered her kissing his cheek so very sweetly.

He tugged the boots on and ran a hand through his hair.

"Baldwin," Simon said, frustration running through his voice as he did so. "Damn it. Everyone can see something is wrong with you. Why won't you talk to us? Any of us? All of us? We could help."

Baldwin turned. Simon was the most careful of their group. He could say something and make it sound kind even if it was a harsh word. If he confessed to his friend, Simon would be nothing but generous and accepting.

But it wouldn't change Baldwin's future. Nor his part in making it.

"I can't," he said. "Now I must find her. Excuse me."

Simon sighed. "She's your perfect match, mate," he called after him. "Meg said she was off toward the lake half an hour ago. Said she needed a walk to clear her mind."

Baldwin ignored him, but his heart leapt as he rushed from the room and toward the woman who so tangled everything in his mind. The one he owed far more to than an awkward fingering in his study chair.

Normally Helena would have been captivated by the beauty of the scene before her. The lake on Baldwin's property was vast, and in the early morning coolness it steamed up fog from its mirrored reflection. Under any other circumstance, she would have drunk it all in, memorizing the moment so she could call it up later and find a little peace.

But today was not normal and the appreciation she would have felt was cut down by more than half as she stood at the water's edge. All she could think about was Baldwin. All she could think about was pleasure.

She'd never experienced such a thing before. But it was...magical. And she wanted more.

"I'm becoming the wanton my uncle always accused me of being," she murmured, shivering as she thought of what kind of reaction Uncle Peter would have if he knew. She'd be on the first boat back to Boston, where she had no one to take her in.

Behind her, she heard a thundering sound and turned to watch a horse barreling down the hill toward the lake. Even from a distance, she recognized the rider. It was Baldwin.

She caught her breath as he brought the animal up short and swung down. He was still wearing his trousers and shirt from the previous night, wrinkled though they were by sleep. He had dark circles beneath his eyes and he looked slightly sick. Not that she was surprised. The poor man had to have a hangover.

And yet he was still here.

"Helena!" he called out as he crossed the distance between them in a few long strides.

She clenched her hands before her and tried to sound calm as she said, "Y-your Grace. What are you doing here?"

He ran a hand through his hair and his gaze darted from hers. "I heard you'd come down here to walk and I know I am disturbing your peace. I know you likely want nothing to do with me after my shocking behavior last night, but I had to find you. I had to speak to you. If you will allow it."

She blinked at the words and the apologetic tone they were spoken in. "I—of course, Baldwin."

He sagged just a fraction, as if he'd actually believed she might turn away from him. Then he held out a hand, like he would touch her. She held her breath for it, wanting it, needing that touch. But before he could, he jerked his hand away.

"I'm so sorry," he whispered.

She shook her head. "Sorry?"

"For my beastly behavior last night," he clarified, his dark eyes holding hers, searching them. She saw his desperation reflected there. His deep regret. It cut her to the bone to see that he was sorry for what they'd done.

"You were not beastly," she said.

He leaned away. "I was, I know I was. I got...bad news during the ball. Something about my finances that I hoped I could resolve, but now seems...well, it's not going to happen. At least not now. I want you to know that I rarely drink to excess. But I was...I was..."

"Desperate," she filled in when he could not.

His head dipped. "Yes, Helena. I was desperate. I thought I could hide in my chamber like some kind of petulant child. To drown my frustrations just this one time. It was churlish and wrong, but I knew I'd be no good company at the party. But when you came in—"

He cut himself off and Helena caught her breath. The pain slashed on his face was so real. "Baldwin," she whispered.

"No, don't offer me comfort," he said, his tone hard. "I do not deserve it. You came to check on me, which was far more kindness than I deserve from you. I rewarded that kindness with markedly ungentlemanly behavior."

Helena shook her head, but he held up a hand and looked like he would continue this self-berating indefinitely. But she could not let it stand. Not now. Not when her own thoughts on the matter were so different.

She stepped forward, uncertain what she could do to stop him from his self-recrimination. She touched his arm and it became clear. She lifted on her tiptoes, caught his cheeks in her palms and kissed him.

For a moment he was stiff, surprised, but then he softened and his arms came around her as he sighed against her lips in surrender. She deepened the kiss, tasting him for just a moment before she blushed and backed away.

He stared at her, but he did not return to talking.

"Stop," she whispered. "Please."

He sighed, ragged and pained. "But—"

"Please, won't you let me speak?" she asked.

She could see him battling with her request. He clearly wanted to confess more. To berate himself further. To try to convince her that he deserved censure for those beautiful moments in his study.

But finally he nodded. "Yes, yes of course."

"If the grass weren't so wet, we could sit together," she said, motioning to the lakeside.

His eyebrows lifted and then he strode off to his horse. He opened the saddlebag and removed a folded blanket, which he spread out before the lake.

"You are always prepared," she said with a laugh as she took her place.

He shook his head. "Not me. I was meant to ride with Simon this morning, so my man put the blanket in, just in case we wished to stop and chat."

"Well, I'm glad for it." They settled onto the blanket and she drew a deep breath. "You didn't do anything wrong last night, Baldwin."

His expression twisted with more of the guilt he carried

around with him constantly. "You are a lady," he insisted.

She sucked in a breath. "No, I'm not. Not by any standard that could be used to judge one such."

He looked confused. "I don't know what you could mean."

She sighed. "You must recall last night. You were not so very drunk, Baldwin."

"Yes," he said slowly. "I recall it and there is nothing that happened that would make me think you're not a lady. Just that I am not a gentleman."

Heat flooded her cheeks, and yet she could stop herself from what she was about to do. To say. She didn't want to. Baldwin had already given so much of himself to her. The only way to comfort him that he was not a monster was to make him understand her own secrets.

"Do you recall when you said that someone had hurt me?" she pressed.

His eyes came shut and he made a low sound in his throat. "Yes," he whispered. "You told me I was right, but I went forward anyway. If I'd been a little more sober—"

"You went forward because I wanted you to," she insisted, catching his hands and forcing him to look at her. "You did not force anything on me. You told me again and again that I could say just a word and you would stop. I never said a word because I didn't want that."

"Still, what I did was wrong," he said softly. "There is the topic of ruination—"

"Do you think you're the only one with secrets, Baldwin?" she interrupted with a shake of her head. "You did not ruin me last night. Not just because you didn't...you didn't...take me. But because even if you had, you would not have been the first to do so."

She watched his face change. He went pale and his expression tightened. Her heart broke as it did, for she knew what would happen next. The censure, the distancing, perhaps even the talk.

"Tell me," he said, and his voice was so soft, so gentle. She heard his empathy and she saw it, too, as his face continued to change as what she said sank in.

This was not a reaction she was accustomed to. She turned her face and looked out at the lake. "He was a suitor of Charity's, back in Boston," she said. "Looking to get her purse, of course. She didn't want him and she had given him a vicious set down. I felt…sorry for him."

He nodded. "Of course you did. You're kind."

"Too kind, it seems," she said with a laugh she had been using to cover up her pain for years. "I found him in the garden, angry and pacing. I tried to be sympathetic, to soften what she'd said. I thought I'd helped, but then he grabbed me and—"

She cut herself off and drew a ragged breath as those images she fought so hard to keep at bay came back. That other man's hands, his mouth, his cruel smile as he took what she did not want to give.

Baldwin's jaw set. "He forced you."

She nodded. "Yes." A tear escaped her eye and she wiped it away. "He took what he desired and he left me in tatters in the gazebo. My cousin found me. She was actually…kind, as she can sometimes be. But once my family found out, it ruined me."

He wrinkled his brow. "But they knew you'd been assaulted."

She shrugged. "Whether I gave or he took, they felt I could have been more prudent. Perhaps they were right at that. I should not have followed him."

"Just as you shouldn't have followed me," he ground out.

She jerked her gaze to him in horror. "Don't you dare compare yourself to him, or what we did last night to what he did three years ago."

"I'm sorry," he said, and it was so very clear that he was. "That was cruel of me to do so after what you've endured. How did you survive?"

"I cried quite a bit," she said with a sigh. "I reached out for support and found no one there to reach back. So I learned to depend upon myself. I learned to ride out all the horrible emotions that come out when I think of that night. I learned to forgive myself and to recognize that it wasn't my fault."

He tilted his head. "You constantly amaze me," he murmured, almost more to himself than to her. "You are beautiful and kind and so damned strong. There is no one in the world like you, Helena. No one in any world."

Heat flooded her cheeks, not just at his compliment, but at the way he looked at her. Like he truly believed she was some singular, wonderful creature. When she was with him, she could almost believe it, too. And that was why what they'd shared mattered so much. Why she didn't want it to be a regret.

"Last night you said something," she said. "Something about how everyone else gets to have what they want."

He ducked his head. "I was rambling, my tongue loosened by one too many drinks."

"But you weren't incorrect. It does sometimes seem like the rest of the world gets to have their dreams and that no matter how hard I try, I cannot. My reward for kindness or hope or survival is to trail after Charity, carrying her train."

He glanced up at her. "I'm so sorry."

"But I'm not." She shook her head. "Oh, I'm bungling this. Let me try to be clearer. All of the steps along my path, the good, the bad, the terrible…they have led me to this moment. To this place. To what happened between us last night. I know you are trying to make yourself the villain in those moments where you touched me, but Baldwin, that was the first time I've felt alive in years."

His jaw set. "Do you mean that?"

She nodded. "I do. You didn't ruin me. And if I had asked you to stop, I have no doubt in my mind that you would have."

"I wish I had not been so addled by drink," he mused, "so that my memories would be crystal clear. I want to savor every moment we shared."

She smiled, this time not forced. He returned the expression, and in that moment they were the only two people in the world. In the universe. She knew only one way to let that stand. Only one thing she wanted more than any other.

Slowly, she scooted toward him on the blanket, holding his gaze as she did so. He caught his breath when she was right next to him.

"You haven't been drinking now," she whispered as she leaned up into him.

"No," he said as he bent his head to hers. "I have not."

Their mouths met and she let out a low sound in her throat. One that released all the need that had been stoked last night. One that spoke of all the desire still burning in her chest. Desire only he could help her stoke and then extinguish.

He deepened the kiss, angling his head to taste her more thoroughly. She lifted her hands to his upper arms, clinging there as she drowned in him and the pleasure his touch brought her.

Finally he pulled back a fraction, his gaze foggy as he stared down at her like he was only just seeing her for the first time. "Helena," he whispered. "I still can't offer you the future you deserve. You know why."

She nodded, pushing away the ache those words caused. "I know," she said. "But you could give me something else, Baldwin. I-I want you. And I know I'll never have this chance again to want someone and have that wanting returned. To trust someone to give me what I shouldn't ask for as a lady."

"What *are* you asking for?" he murmured as he traced her cheek with the tip of his finger.

She caught her breath and forced herself to be brave. "You, Baldwin. I want you."

CHAPTER FOURTEEN

Baldwin burned as she said those words. The ones he knew were coming, the ones that made him come back to life after years of being dead, buried in pain and betrayal and failure.

This ache that he felt for her, it only grew deeper now that he knew her story. Now that he heard her strength.

"You're asking for an...affair?" he asked, wishing his voice didn't waver.

Her cheeks brightened with high color, and he shuddered as he recalled the same heat entering them when he brought her to completion the night before. Even slightly wobbly, it was a powerful memory he savored far more than he should.

She wrung her hands and he felt her struggle. Men of their sphere were allowed to explore their desires. Expected to, even. It did not harm their future, assuming one was prudent about it.

He recognized how different desire was for a woman. Ladies were very often taught that desire was a point of shame. That pleasure was not to be expected. And if they were ruined...

Well, Helena's situation summed up the consequences perfectly. She had been assaulted, but the blame was laid at her feet. Somehow she'd had the strength to pull herself through the trauma of that night, but she had suffered for it.

The idea that she would trust him, gift him, with her reawakening...well, that was the most powerful thing of all.

"An affair," she repeated softly, as if hearing those words

in her own voice would help her decide if that was her path. "Y-yes," she stammered at last, and looked at him with clear eyes. "I do want that."

He moved even closer to her on the blanket. Now he felt the delicate warmth of her skin against his. Now he felt the way she trembled ever so slightly. He traced his thumb across her cheek and she shivered with the touch.

"You know what I can and can't offer you," he said, hating that he had to say those words. "The idea of taking advantage of you is abhorrent."

She held his stare. "Everyone else gets what they want, Baldwin. I know the limitations. I understand the reasons why. But if we both agree, if we both understand, then no one will take advantage, will they? And this is that chance to get this one little thing that we want."

With that statement, she was a siren. He was a sailor, only he saw the rocks, saw the danger. He saw it all and he didn't care. Because what she offered was so fucking sweet.

He tilted her face up and kissed her once more. She opened to him right away, and her enthusiasm dissolved any remaining hesitance he might have. He wanted her. She was offering him a chance to have her. And with that chance, he would not only take. He would make sure that this affair was only pleasure to her. That it helped to mute her painful memories. That it would create new ones they could both recall after it was…after it was over.

He shoved that future away and laid her back on the blanket. He rolled to cover her and shivered when her arms came around his back in welcome and surrender. He had needs, such powerful needs. But right now he didn't care about those. He wanted her to enjoy this.

He deepened the kiss and she let out a shuddering sigh against his lips. He drove inside, tasting every inch of her mouth, thrusting with his tongue like he would eventually do with his body. When he felt her relax against him, it was only then that he touched her. He let his hand glide up her side and cupped one breast through her silky gown.

She arched beneath him with a gasp that broke their kiss, and he drew back to watch her in her pleasure. Last night he'd been too tipsy to really gauge all her reactions well. Right now he reveled in the way her eyes widened and her pupils dilated. In the way her breath hitched when his thumb traced the outline of her nipple. In how she lifted her hips to his, and he doubted she even knew she was doing it because she was lost in his touch.

"I want to take you, Helena," he murmured as he kept circling that nipple over and over again. "You cannot fully understand how much I want that."

She gave a jerky nod. "I think I understand a little."

He smiled. "I'm not doing it here."

Her face fell. "No?"

"I want this affair, I do. But I recognize fully what a gift you are giving me to offer it. After what you've experienced, I'm not going to treat you like some scandalous tup that means nothing. It means a great deal."

He had continued to swirl his thumb around her nipple as he spoke, and she was nodding, but he could see the pleasure was distracting. Good. He wanted her distracted by pleasure every time he touched her. He wanted her trembling with it. Weak with it. She deserved that.

She deserved far more.

"Right now I'm going to make you come," he promised.

She stared at him. "Come?"

"Like last night," he whispered. "When the pleasure got so big that it couldn't be contained. When you coated my fingers with all that slick release."

Her cheeks darkened again with that wicked description. He was a little surprised at himself for giving it. He was a gentleman. It was left to silver-tongued rogues like Robert to burn a lady's ears with naughty words.

But Helena inspired him.

"I was…overcome when you touched me," she admitted softly. "I've never felt anything like it."

"Good," he said. "You're about to again."

He inched down her body, kissing her through her clothing as he did so. He pushed at her skirts, raising them until he could part the opening of her drawers. He caught his breath.

Last night he had not looked at her. Even if he had, he would have been too drunk to appreciate her fully. Today he did. She was slick with desire already, and he couldn't help himself. He lowered his head and placed a gentle kiss to her.

"Baldwin!" she cried out, half sitting up on the blanket to stare at him.

He looked up at her from between her legs. "I'm going to kiss you here. Lick you. And if you allow me to do that, I promise you that the pleasure of last night will seem muted in comparison."

Her lips parted and the sweetest expression of innocent shock rolled across her face. Like she couldn't image that was true. Still, as much as he wanted to dive right into this act, he had to be mindful of what she had endured.

He never wanted to hurt her. Ever.

"Hear me, Helena," he whispered. "*You* have all the control when it comes to this. When it comes to any way I touch you. The moment you say no, I will stop. I don't care how far I've gone or what you've said yes to in the past. Your *no* ceases everything." He chuckled. "Even if it kills me."

She continued to stare at him. "You would—you would do that?"

"Of course," he said. "You are not a toy to be used by me and thrown aside. We both know the circumstances, the blockades, the future that we cannot avoid. But I want this to give you pleasure. I want it to be something you look back on with joy. This affair is for you, Helena, as much as it is for me."

She swallowed hard and then she nodded. "Thank you."

"Now, may I?" he asked, tilting his head toward her sex.

Her lips parted, her uncertainty still clear. But then she swallowed hard and said, "Yes. I trust you, Baldwin."

He recognized just how hard that trust was to give and

vowed, if only to himself, to never make her regret giving it. Gently, he placed a hand on each of her thighs and pressed her open. He rested on his stomach between her legs, then stroked his fingers over her sex.

She made a garbled sound of pleasure and her legs fell open wider. He smiled as he gently parted the folds of her sex, and leaned in to lick her once more.

Helena jolted at the unexpected and powerful sensation of Baldwin's tongue tracing her in the most intimate way possible. The idea that he would had been confusing, but now…now that he was actually doing it, she understood. This was magical.

Better still, he seemed to enjoy it just as much, for he dove into the act with great determination and gusto. He was relentless, dragging his tongue across her opening and then swirling it around the same place where he'd touched her last night. And just as she had all those hours ago, she found herself grinding against him in time to his strokes, reaching for that pleasure she had found with him before.

Talented and focused as he was, it didn't take long to get there. They found a rhythm together, something hard and fast that made her legs shake as she pressed her heels into the blanket. He stroked and stroked with the flat of his tongue, and she couldn't stop the little keening cries that escaped her lips and drifted away on the soft breezes coming from the lake.

The pressure built, just as it had the night before. A gathering pleasure that was so much like a storm. She wanted it. She needed it more than breath or food or water. She was desperate for it, and just as she reached the peak of that need, he sucked her and she shattered.

He continued to lick her as she thrashed against him, clenching the blanket, twisting to escape the pleasure, grinding to find more. It went on and on, far longer than the previous night. Those ripples multiplied until she was weak from it. Only then did he lift his mouth from her and grant her respite from the powerful, uncontrollable sensation.

He crawled up the length of her body and kissed her. She drank deeply of him, tasting an earthy sweet flavor on his tongue that jolted even more desire through her. It was her flavor from that secret place she'd been taught was dirty and wrong.

It didn't taste wrong. What he'd done hadn't felt wrong either. It had felt…wonderful. And he'd been so gentle, so giving and caring that her memories hadn't plagued her when he touched her. In fact, nothing had troubled her at all in those sweet, sensual moments.

He smoothed her skirts down and rolled to lie beside her, gently resting his hand on her stomach. "That was much better when I am fully sober," he said with a smile that brightened his somber face considerably.

She laughed. "Sober or drunk, you sweep me away in ways I didn't know were possible."

He curled his hand against her. "You deserve that pleasure, Helena. And it is very much my pleasure to give it to you."

She frowned and looked down his body. Just as she'd seen last night, she was well aware of the swollen reminder that he had not found his pleasure with her either time he had touched her.

"What about you?" she asked.

He arched a brow. "Are you trying to tempt me, Miss Monroe?"

"I hope I do tempt you," she said.

He caught her hand and gently dragged it down his body until she cupped the hardness of him. "You do," he promised. "But when I resolve this, I want it to be buried in your body. And I only want to do that when I have the time to do it properly."

"In the midst of a country party, that could be challenging."

He shrugged as he released her hand. "I'm very good at challenges." For a moment they lay like that and then he glanced up behind him, toward the house that was hidden over the hill.

"Much as I would like to lie here with you all day, it's getting later in the morning. Soon the others will rise."

She moaned as she buried her head in his shoulder. "I don't want to go back to reality."

He laughed as he smoothed a hand over her hair. "Neither do I, I promise you. But we must."

She nodded slowly and then lifted her head with a smile for him. "Thank you for the fantasy, though."

"Thank you," he replied before he kissed her once more.

She wanted to sink into it. To surrender to it and to him. But he didn't allow it. With a groan, he pulled back and then got to his feet. She watched him straighten himself before he offered her a hand to help her up. She took it and did her best to fix her dress. Beneath it her drawers were slightly cockeyed, but she wasn't about to fix those.

"Walk with me," he said as they started up the hill to where his horse had gone to graze. He caught the reins as they passed the animal and together they climbed up the hill.

She sighed as the house appeared in the distance. Reality loomed, as it always would. Now she began to think of consequences and futures and loss and everything else.

"You said you got bad news last night," she said. "Is there anything I can do to help?"

He sent her a side look. "You just did."

She shook her head. "You pretend with everyone else, Baldwin, please don't pretend with me."

She saw the air go out of him, his shoulders slumped, and for a moment the weight he carried was so obvious. "It was just bad news about the debts I told you about."

She frowned. "The ones you had not been able to discover."

He nodded. "Yes. Someone has...bought them all."

They were almost to the house now, and she stopped on the path to face him. "One person bought them all? Who?"

"That was the bad news—I do not know." He sighed and looked toward the house. "It cannot be for any good reason, though."

She tended to agree, but saying so would not relieve him. Instead she reached out and touched his arm. "You do not know anything for certain yet. Have faith, Baldwin. You are too good not to have the best of things happen for you."

He stared down at her, and for a moment she thought he might kiss her. She wanted him to, even though she stole a glance up at the house where anyone could be watching. He did the same and sighed.

"Thank you," he said. "You were exactly what I needed to clear my mind."

"If I did so even a little, then I'm glad," she said. With a sigh, she stepped away. "I must go inside. The morning is getting late, and any moment my cousin will wake and come barreling into the sitting room to demand I assist her."

His brow wrinkled. "The sitting room?"

Helena shrugged. "She wanted the bed all to herself. I sleep on the settee."

His jaw set and she saw the flash of anger that crossed his face. Intense and entirely on her behalf. "That little—"

Her eyes widened and she shook her head. "Don't. It isn't worth it."

"I knew I should have given you your own chamber," he said. "I thought the beautiful view would please you and—"

She tilted her head. "You chose the room with the view for—for me?"

"Of course," he said with no hesitation. "You did not think it was for Charity, did you?" He snorted his derision.

Her skin grew hot with pleasure and she bent her head. "Oh, well, I…I should go in. Thank you. Good morning."

He watched her as she turned and scurried into the house away from him. Away from all they'd done together by the lake. She had no idea where this affair was going.

All she knew was that she hoped it would continue.

CHAPTER FIFTEEN

When Helena entered the chamber a few moments after parting from Baldwin, she found Charity waiting. Her cousin glared at her and snapped, "And just where have you been?"

Helena tried to slow her suddenly racing heart and put on the brightest smile she could manage. "I woke early and thought I'd take a walk around the grounds. Good morning, Perdy."

Charity's maid lifted her gaze from her work fastening Charity's gown and smiled slightly. Helena felt for her. Poor Perdy had to deal with Charity and her moods on a more regular basis than Helena did. Just the past few months had been more than enough for her.

"Did you?" Charity said, arching a brow. "By yourself?"

Helena shifted. Here was a tricky situation. She certainly wasn't going to tell her cousin what had really happened this morning, but if she lied about seeing Baldwin and someone told Charity, it would only make things worse. Her cousin already seemed far too interested in the duke and how Helena interacted with him.

"I did bump into the Duke of Sheffield. He was out on a morning ride," she admitted. "We walked back together."

Charity tilted her head, and then she smiled. "And did you talk about me?"

"Yes," Helena said with a tight smile of her own. Not untrue, though she doubted Charity would like the tone or the topic of that conversation. She still blushed when she thought of Baldwin defending her, of him choosing this lovely room for *her*.

"Good," Charity said. "We could yet make use of your odd little friendship with him and his family."

Helena came farther into the room and sat down near Charity. Perdy was just finishing the dressing, and soon her cousin would take a place at the dressing table to have her hair done.

"How so?" Helena asked.

"He's very handsome," Charity said. She was holding Helena's gaze far too evenly now. "Don't you think?"

Helena stopped breathing. She'd known Charity all her life—they'd grown up together—and was well aware of the little twists of Charity's mouth and tones of her voice. Her cousin was digging for information. Trying to find out things that Helena didn't want to share.

Charity obviously had suspicions. Ones that could be very dangerous considering the agreement Helena had just entered into with Baldwin.

She cleared her throat. "He is one of many handsome men at this gathering. The Duke of Tyndale is also quite well put together. And there are a few others with lesser titles who could not be called ugly."

"I wasn't asking about *them*, I was asking about *him*." Charity turned her dressing table chair so it was facing Helena and then deposited herself into it, forcing Perdy to wedge herself between table and chair to fix Charity's hair.

"He is handsome," Helena said softly.

"I like him, I think," Charity continued. "At least as much as anyone else. He approached me after he saw me dancing with Grifford. Maybe he was jealous of our connection."

Helena tried to remain calm. "You have a connection with the Earl of Grifford? The man you once complained was so old?"

Charity shrugged. "He has grown on me. But he's no duke. What would you think of my pursuing Sheffield?"

Everything in the room suddenly slowed to half time as Helena stared at her cousin. She knew Baldwin didn't particularly like Charity. In any other circumstance that fact would have made her comfortable that this fancy of her cousin's would lead to nothing.

But she also knew Baldwin's situation. And her uncle Peter had made certain that Charity was in the best financial position of almost any girl out Season, either here in England or in Boston.

That dowry wasn't something Baldwin could ignore. And so the idea sat in Helena's stomach like a rock.

"I think it would be..." She cleared her throat around the lump there. "I'm certain it would be a beneficial match for you both."

"I agree." Charity sent a dark look at her maid. "Gracious, Perdy, you are tugging!"

Helena squeezed her eyes shut as Charity snapped at the poor maid. Her heart had never hurt more in her entire life. Thinking about Charity pursuing Baldwin and him being forced to consider it...

After what they'd just shared, she could barely stand the idea.

"Get my necklace, won't you, Helena?" Charity said, motioning to the jewelry box on the table across the room.

Helena shook off her thoughts and went to do as she'd been told. Because that's what she did. There was no other choice.

Baldwin drew a long breath, closed his eyes and tilted his head up toward the sun. For just a moment, a sense of peace came over him. It was the first time he'd been alone since his mother's suggestion that they arrange this country party, and now he relished the moment. Soon enough he would have to go back inside. Soon enough he'd have to return his mind to debts and prospects, and he'd have to be near Helena and want her so much that it actually hurt.

But for now he was—

"Your Grace?"

He let out a small sigh before he opened his eyes and watched as one of his mother's prospects came down the lane in the garden toward him. Lady Winifred, daughter of the Earl of Snodgrass. Fifteen thousand pounds and that damned racehorse. The facts rolled through his head, and he flinched at how mercenary he'd become. He looked a little closer. She was not an unattractive young lady. Dark hair, brown eyes, pretty face. She just wasn't the person he wanted.

He rose from his seat on the bench and forced a smile. "Lady Winifred," he said. "Come down for a walk, have you?"

She nodded and said, "Your mother and I were talking about my love for roses, so she sent me down to look at yours."

"My mother," he repeated slowly. He turned his gaze up toward the terrace above and saw the duchess standing there. He frowned at her heavy hand and at the way she waved at him before she had the decency to turn away and leave her machinations to play out.

"Yes," Lady Winifred said. "She was quite insistent and I think she planned to go with me, but then she was distracted by a household matter.

"Of course she was. Well, I would be remiss if I did not offer to show you around the grounds myself, then." He offered her an arm and she took it without hesitation. He tensed as she did so, hating how he felt...nothing for her. No spark, no interest. Just nothing.

Because she wasn't Helena. Once again that thought pressed into his mind. He had to force it out again as they began to walk through the garden, his companion talking on and on about roses. Types. Colors. Scents. Origins.

Great God, this would be his life. Endless talk of roses as he desperately tried to make fifteen thousand pounds and a racehorse stretch to fill his empty coffers.

"Your Grace?" she said.

He blinked and glanced down at her. "My most sincere apologies, my lady. I was distracted and it was very rude of me. I think you were discussing the moss rose."

"I was," she admitted. "But I was about to say that your roses have all bloomed quite early this year."

He looked around at the budding beauties his mother and grandmother had both loved so well. "I suppose it is a bit early, yes."

Lady Winifred tilted her head. "It's bad luck, you know. For them to bloom early."

Baldwin stifled a laugh that held no humor. "Well, sometimes the only luck a man has is bad luck."

Lady Winifred looked at him with a confused expression. Not curious, just uncertain. But before they could continue their talk, the Countess of Snodgrass came down the path and smiled at the pair. "There you are, Winifred. And hello, Your Grace."

Baldwin nodded. "My lady."

"Winifred, you've been roaming through the duke's gardens for almost half an hour now. You do not want to get too tan. A gentleman doesn't like a lady who is too sun-kissed—isn't that right, Your Grace?"

Baldwin released Winifred, who returned to her mother's side. He felt a great sense of relief when she did so. "I would not be able to speak for all gentlemen," he offered.

Lady Snodgrass giggled and Winifred blushed. "Good afternoon, Your Grace. We'll see you at supper tonight."

The pair turned and walked away, leaving Baldwin to sag against the nearest tree in exhaustion.

"Good afternoon."

He froze, his heart leaping as it had not when he was standing with the other young lady. He knew that voice. And he turned to find Helena standing a few feet away, watching him carefully.

"Helena," he whispered, her name a prayer, a plea, a balm. "I'm so glad it's you and not some other woman my mother is marching down from the main house for me."

Helena shifted slightly. "Yes, I saw you with Lady Winifred. She is one of the...options then?"

Baldwin stared up at the house where the young woman and her mother had gone. "Yes," he said softly. "She is, I suppose."

"Well, she's pretty," Helena offered, her tone very careful.

He turned on her with a grin. "Are you now playing my matchmaker?"

She did not return the smile. "I think that would be too difficult."

He nodded. "Yes. All of this is...difficult."

"For both of us, I would imagine. You didn't like her at all?"

Baldwin shrugged. "It isn't about liking or not liking. She's a nice enough young woman. I just don't feel...anything when I'm with her."

Helena swallowed hard. "I see."

"Not like when I'm with you," he murmured, and moved toward her a step.

She caught her breath and he saw her pupils dilate with desire. He loved to see that blossom in her, rather like the flowers Lady Winifred had been going on and on about.

"We're so close to the house," Helena whispered. "Anyone could see."

"A valid point," he said, and offered her an arm. "Walk with me? I'd much prefer your company."

She looked like she would argue. Probably make a point that what they were doing was dangerous and wrong and not conducive to acceptance of the future either of them would soon face.

Instead, she sighed and said, "Of course. You know I couldn't say no."

She took his arm, and this time there was plenty for him to feel. Warmth and pleasure, desire and desperation. He was aware of every part of her that pressed to him, of the feel of each finger that curled into the crook of his elbow. He felt it all and he reveled in it.

"So what did you talk about?" she asked.

He glanced down at her as they began to walk farther into the garden, farther away from the house and whatever prying eyes there might see. "You really want to know?"

"I don't know," she muttered. "Part of me does want to know. Part of me doesn't. All of me is jealous and I hate myself for it."

He shook his head. "You needn't be jealous. Lady Winifred is quite a fan of flowers and all I heard about was roses, roses, roses for half an hour."

She glanced up at him. "That's all she could think of to say to you?"

"You sound incredulous. I may just bring out the dullest of subjects in people," he said with a laugh that lightened everything about his mood.

He only felt that way with her, it seemed.

She smiled. "You may at that. I wouldn't have picked that subject to talk to you about."

"What subject would you have chosen?" he asked, and guided her into the covered gazebo.

She looked around with a blush, and he could see her mind turning. Working out the same problem he'd been pondering. Would they be safe enough here for a kiss? Nothing more, of course, there was too much danger. But could he kiss her?

She bit her lip as she released his arm and backed away. "My cousin told me she plans to pursue you."

All of Baldwin's happy, playful thoughts faded from his mind and he stared at Helena in horror. "Charity?"

"Yes, she is my only cousin who could pursue you, I think, since all the others are back in America," she said, turning away to pace the gazebo. "She told me this morning after I returned from—from when you…"

She didn't look at him, but placed both hands on the half wall of the gazebo and leaned there like the weight of the world was on her shoulders.

"I see," he murmured. "You know I don't want her."

"You don't want any of them," Helena said, glancing at him. "But we both know the danger. Charity has a huge dowry. It may even be bigger than everyone is whispering about. I recognize you'd have to consider it."

His stomach turned. "Hear me, Helena. I could not consider your cousin, not if she had a hundred thousand pounds, or a million."

High color touched her cheeks and she smiled slightly. "Don't be silly. *I* would marry her for a million pounds."

He recognized what she was doing, how she was trying to diffuse the situation through humor. And it worked. He smiled despite himself and reached out to take her hand.

"Let's not talk about her," he said. "I have such little time with you, I don't want to waste it talking about Charity or Lady Winifred or roses."

"Then you choose the topic, since you've suffered so today," she said, another teasing smile tilting her lips.

Lips he wanted to kiss so very desperately. Only a kiss would lead to other things right now.

So instead, he guided her so they could sit together on the bench in the gazebo's center. "Tell me about your friends at home."

He had expected her to brighten at that topic, but instead her body went stiff next to his and her jaw tightened.

"I'm sorry," he said, holding her hand a little tighter. "I did not mean to find a painful subject for you."

"It's not your fault," she said softly. "The truth of my ruination came out amongst my friends. I had confided in my closest friend, needing someone to talk to. Instead, she told the rest and they…they turned away from me. The scandal grew, its facts twisted to be even worse and…well, I wouldn't want to return to Boston, I don't think."

Baldwin shook his head slowly, filled with disbelief. "Those do not sound like friends," he growled. "I cannot imagine my own set of friends not standing by my side."

"Is that why you lie to them about your situation?" she asked, gently but pointedly.

He stared at her. "A fair argument," he said. "And not one we need to hash over again. But Helena, please know that the friendships you're forging with Emma, Meg, Charlotte and Adelaide, they are far truer. A better group of women I have never known in my life."

Helena shifted. "I thought my own friends would see me through, too. I don't want the duchesses to know the truth."

There was a hint of desperation to her tone. A lilt of terror and sadness and grief that twisted Baldwin's gut. He could no longer hold himself back. He cupped her chin, leaned in and brushed his lips over hers.

She made a soft little sound of surrender in her throat that drove him mad, but he didn't deepen the kiss or demand more from her. This wasn't about possession or desire. It was about comfort. Support. And emotions he refused to name because they could come to nothing.

He drew back and held her gaze evenly. "I will not tell your secret, Helena. I would never betray you like that. But I do want to say that I promise you that your new friends would never turn on you."

"But they wouldn't understand," she whispered.

"Adelaide and Emma would," he said softly. "Both of them narrowly escaped the same fate you experienced."

Her eyes widened. "Adelaide and Emma?" she repeated.

"Attacked by the same man, at different times," he said, his jaw tightening as he thought of those stories James and Graham had told. At the time he'd been angry enough, but now he was enraged. Now he could picture what Helena had endured, and it shattered his heart.

"The same man," she said, her eyes widening with terror.

"He's dead now," he reassured her. "I'm only trying to say that what happened to them was not their fault. And I know they would understand what you went through if you chose to tell them the truth."

She sighed heavily and stared off into the garden, though it was with distant eyes that didn't seem to truly see. "I'll think about it, Baldwin. I will. It might be...nice to have friends to confide in who understood."

"You've been dealing with this on your own for so long," he encouraged. "I hope you will consider it."

She looked around and then briefly rested her head against his shoulder. Warmth spread through his whole body, and he wrapped his arms around her as she sagged against him. She trusted him to be her strength in that moment, and his body swelled with pride...and a desire to protect her for the rest of her life.

Only he couldn't. And she seemed to recall that at the same time he did, for she sat up and smiled at him. It was a shaky expression, not entirely believable.

"Now we should go back," she said. "Charity was taking a nap, but she'll wake soon and I will have duties to perform for her."

He nodded and stood to offer her his arm a second time. As she took it and he guided her back into the garden, he said, "The good thing is that now I can tell you facts about every rose that ever existed as we make our way back to the house."

She laughed, a full belly laugh that seemed to jolt him in an electric way. "I cannot wait, Your Grace. One can never know too much about roses, I've heard."

"Not true," he teased. "By the time I'm done, you will modify that statement. Now, let us consider the centifolia..."

CHAPTER SIXTEEN

Normally Helena loved breakfast. She'd never been a picky eater, and Baldwin's cook was talented in every way. But this morning, she found that everything before her tasted of sawdust and even the smells turned her stomach. But the reason had nothing to do with the quality of the food.

She glanced down the table and watched as Baldwin leaned toward one of the eligible misses who currently surrounded him. His prospects, as she knew he called them. The women from whom he would pick a bride. Including her cousin, despite all his arguments to the contrary.

And today he seemed determined to connect with those women. She wasn't angry. Of course she understood. But oh, how it hurt to look at it. To see him talk with those women and know that one day he would touch one of them the same way he'd touched her.

"Miss Monroe, you do look lovely today."

She jolted and turned to look at Baldwin's mother. The Duchess of Sheffield had taken a place beside her a few moments earlier, but had been engaged in conversation with the Duchess of Abernathe until this moment. Now she smiled at Helena.

"Thank you, Your Grace," Helena said with a blush. Her dress was not as pretty or fancy as some of the other ladies' gowns. By design, she supposed. Charity was very stingy about hand-me-downs. She generally only gave Helena the plainest items in her closet. Still, she liked the color, a happy blue with a spring-green overlay.

"My daughter and her friends speak so highly of you," the duchess continued. "Charlotte has so enjoyed having you here."

"Her Grace is very kind," Helena said. "I very much enjoy spending time with her and the other duchesses."

"Tell me more about yourself," the Duchess of Sheffield pressed. "Charlotte says you are a great reader."

"I do enjoy a good book, yes. To be taken away to a whole other world, to lose oneself for a few hours. It is my favorite thing."

The duchess nodded. "I've always felt the same way. We will have to compare reading lists, as I am in the mood for something good."

"Certainly," Helena said. "I'd be happy to share. Actually, I finished a very good book on the trip out to Sheffield. My cousin is not a reader, so if you'd like it…"

The duchess gave her a warm smile. "That would be lovely, thank you." She shifted slightly and her gaze moved to Baldwin. There was no mistaking the worry she felt. The pressure. All of Helena's warm feelings faded as reality returned, as it always did.

"You are…concerned for your son?" she asked carefully.

The duchess looked at her slowly, one eyebrow arched. "Am I so obvious?"

Helena shrugged. "Only if one is observant."

Now the duchess held her stare. "And you are when it comes to Baldwin, I think."

Helena's breath hitched. It seemed she wasn't the only observant one. She thought they had been careful, but the shift in the Duchess of Sheffield's demeanor told her it wasn't careful enough.

"I'm a bit on the fringes, that is all, Your Grace," she said. "I notice everyone."

The duchess nodded, but her expression remained as

focused as before. Helena had not diffused its intensity or understanding. "I'm a mother," the duchess said slowly. "It is my prerogative to worry about my children. Charlotte is so happily settled now, so I'm afraid my concerns all shift to Baldwin."

"I should not have pried," Helena said softly. "I apologize."

"No, it's clear you are a...you're a very good woman," the duchess said. "No one could spend a moment with you and not like you. You seem to care for my children, as well, so I appreciate that." She looked off at her son again. "Baldwin has responsibilities, Miss Monroe. Life is often not fair in that way, but it is what it is. We must accept. We must...we must accept it."

Helena stared down at her plate, the food now turning her stomach even further. The duchess wasn't just talking anymore. This was a statement directed at Helena. A gentle statement, yes. One kindly put, but it did its job nonetheless. She was discouraging Helena from a pursuit of Baldwin.

She felt the sting of tears in her eyes. The discomfort of embarrassment. The faint resonance of loss. But she could not let those things show. As always, she had to pretend.

In fact, the only place where she didn't have to pretend were in those stolen moments with the very man she had just been told could not be hers. And time was running out on what they could share.

Which made her desperate, indeed.

Baldwin stretched his back as he entered his chamber, where he actually smiled at his bed. What he wanted more than anything was to sleep off what had turned into very long day. He'd spent his entire afternoon with the prospects. His mother had made certain of that. She hadn't even been particularly subtle about it.

And they were fine. They were all *fine*. Nothing truly wrong with a one of them, save perhaps Charity, who he didn't like at all. The rest had one common issue. They weren't Helena. Helena, who he kept looking for in every crowd. Helena, who had been kept just as busy as he had, by her wretched uncle and cousin. If he didn't know better, he would have thought his mother and Helena's family had coordinated their efforts to keep them apart.

Only his mother wouldn't work in league with Peter Shephard. She had some standards, even in her desperation.

He moved to ring the bell and call his valet, but before he could do so, there was a rustling behind him. He turned and was shocked when Helena, herself, stepped from the shadows in the corner of his room.

Her face was pale, her eyes wide and her hands trembled at her sides as she whispered, "I—should I have come?"

He didn't answer, not with words. He could find none when his emotions and his desires were swelling up inside of him. Instead, he crossed the room in a few long strides, gathered her against him and kissed her. She immediately softened, winding her arms around his neck, gasping when he caught her backside and drew her even closer.

"I have great hopes that this isn't a dream," he murmured against her lips.

She smiled. "It isn't," she reassured him as he began to kiss her neck. "But it isn't quite reality, either."

He drew back and looked down at her. So lovely and so perfect and yet so out of reach. He cleared his throat. "Then let's celebrate the fantasy while we can. But first, a question."

She nodded. "Of course."

"What about your cousin?"

"Charity is snoring in her bed, believing with every fiber of her being that I am asleep on the settee in her dressing room. She's never been one to get up in the middle of the night, so we are safe in that regard."

"Good," he said, backing her toward his bed slowly. "Then

I can keep you all night. Or nearly so."

She shivered and he paused, forcing himself to recall her past, feeling the potential for fear and anxiety. He took a deep breath and leaned with her against the high edge of his bed.

"I want to make love to you, Helena," he whispered. "I want that more than anything. But not if it causes you grief. So tell me, is that what you want?"

She didn't hesitate, but nodded immediately. That put some ease into his heart. As did her words when she said, "All I can think about is you, Baldwin. It won't last. It can't. But I want tonight."

"Good," he said, and slid his hands to where her simple gown fastened in the front. He never broke her gaze as he slipped each button free. "But if you need me to stop or wait or go slowly, I want you to tell me. We have all night. And I want to make it perfect."

Helena shuddered as Baldwin parted her gown and revealed the plain chemise beneath. His warm fingers slid beneath the fabric and slowly eased it from her shoulders, down her arms, her hips, and let it fall around her feet.

She shifted slightly, uncomfortable about being seen in such a revealed state. Her shift was thin cotton, washed too many times, and she knew it was almost see-through in some places. Under that she wore a pair of drawers, the pleated edges of which peeked out from beneath the chemise. She felt her skin getting hot as he just stared at her, silent. Reverent, even.

"You are so beautiful. I want to memorize every line of you. I want to burn this image in my mind forever so I never lose it, no matter what age and infirmity bring."

She shivered at those sweet words. And again when he tucked a finger beneath each thin strap of her chemise and tugged it down, too. Inch by inch her skin was exposed, lower and lower until her breasts were bared and kissed by the warm air in the room.

She turned her head, unable to meet his eyes anymore.

"So lovely," he muttered, more to himself, it seemed, than to her. As her chemise fluttered to join her gown, he lifted a hand and gently cupped her bare breast. He stroked his thumb over her nipple and electric pleasure sizzled through her veins until she gasped in surprise.

He slid a hand beneath her knees and lifted her onto his bed. She settled against the pillows and watched as he stepped away and stripped open his jacket buttons. He cast it aside, the same with his waistcoat. He unwrapped his cravat and unbuttoned his shirt. Pulling it from his trousers, he tugged the contraption over his head and her world just…stopped.

He was something. Broad-shouldered, perfectly muscled, with just a sprinkling of chest hair that made a path into his trouser waist. She had not had much experience with naked men. Her attacker hadn't undressed. Her only points of reference were garden statues that made her eyes boggle.

This was different.

He tugged his boots off, then moved back toward her, leaving his trousers in place, just as her drawers were. He took a spot beside her on the bed, rolling to his side to face her.

"Still fine?" he asked.

She nodded. "Yes. You must understand, Baldwin, what happened, I've already been broken from it. But broken bones heal stronger. I'm that."

"Yes, I can see that's true. I admire it enormously." He met her gaze. "It doesn't mean that I won't take care with you. Not just because of your past, but because you are lovely and wonderful and you deserve to be—" He leaned in and traced his tongue around her bare nipple. "—worshipped," he finished.

She arched beneath him, in wonder at all the amazing things this man could make her feel and want and do. Tonight she wanted everything. It might be the only time she experienced such bliss.

There was no turning back from her needs now.

If he sensed that surrender, he made it clear by lifting her breast a little and going back to licking. *Sucking.* Little bursts of pleasure shot through her every time he did so, mimicking the way her body fluttered when he touched her intimately. This wasn't release, exactly, but it drew her toward it. Muted pleasure that promised so much more.

"There is nothing like your taste," he whispered against her skin. "I'll never forget it."

She lifted to him, her fingers combing into his hair as he sucked a bit harder, right to the edge of pain, but never over it. Just enough to make her feel alive and wanted and free.

As he pleasured her, he slid a free hand down the apex of her body, stroking his fingers over her bare skin until he came to the drawstring of her pantalettes. He pulled away from her breast and lifted his gaze to hers.

She was shaking. She knew he could feel it. Anticipation pulsed through her, but also anxiousness. Also fear. No matter how long it had been, the fear fluttered back and settled in her chest.

He glanced down, and together they watched his fingers work to untie the bow on the drawstring. With a few expert flicks of his wrist, he untangled the string and let the tension off her waistband. Slowly his hand slid in, over her stomach, across her mound. Her legs opened, granting him access to her sex once more.

He stroked there, sliding the wetness of her body across her sex. "It hurt before," he said.

She sucked in her breath, trying not to go back to that dark night and the man who had stolen her innocence and her dreams in one cruel act. "Yes," she admitted.

"It won't tonight," he promised. "Tonight is about you and your pleasure. If you trust me, I will make every effort to wipe away the past and make this time, this first time, something you do not regret."

She gasped as his finger breached her slightly. "I already

regret nothing," she managed to croak out as the pleasure he could so easily generate began to build. "Please, just…just give me this."

He gently pumped his finger in and out for a few strokes, then pulled away, leaving her body clenching against nothingness. He took himself off the bed and she stared as he unfastened his trousers and shucked them off in one smooth motion.

Her eyes boggled. Half-naked was one thing, fully naked another. She hardly knew where to look. Trim hips? Heavily muscled thighs? Or that thing between his legs. A cock, she'd heard it called. It was hard and jutted toward his stomach.

He said nothing but moved to the bed. He caught the edging of her drawers and tugged them off, tossing them over his shoulder and leaving her as naked as he was.

They stared at each other. His face contained as much wonder as she knew her own did, although a man like him had to have had lovers before. She was merely the next in a line, so why he appeared so enthralled was beyond her.

He moved closer, placing a hand on her calf. He watched her face as he drew his fingers up and up, skin on skin in places where no other person had ever touched her. Now he brought her to life, making her ultra-aware of everything he did to her.

He moved to the bed again, but his time he caged his body over hers. She gasped as his mouth covered hers. But kissing was comfortable, it didn't make her afraid. Soon, she sank into the stunning desire he created as he brushed his lips against hers. Anxiety faded as he continued to kiss and kiss her, replaced by the warm desire that bubbled up in her entire body.

He drew back and she felt him shift, using his knees to part her legs a little farther, wedging himself into that snug spot so she felt the hard length of him just brush against her sex.

His gaze held hers, steady and calming, and he pushed forward. She felt him breach her, and immediately she tensed against the impending violation and the pain that would follow. No matter what he said, she knew what it would be like.

He stopped immediately and looked down at her with concern. "Gently, Helena," he whispered. "Trust me."

She drew a few long breaths. Trust him. That was easy in some areas, but in this...not as much. Still, she breathed, slow and deep, willing her body to relax. To cede control to him because he promised he would not take advantage of it. Bit by bit she relaxed, and it was only then that he moved again.

He stretched her with every inch, and she kept waiting for the pain. But it didn't come. If anything, it was a delicious sensation of being filled up. His cock hit her in spots she didn't know existed, and the pleasure she had felt before when he touched her or licked her murmured below the surface, whispering promises she didn't know were possible.

Finally he fully seated inside of her and rested his forehead against hers. His breath came short and his hands gripped into fists as he pressed them into the pillow around her head. He was fighting for control, to be easy for her.

It meant the world.

"I want to move," he ground out, his voice rough with passion. "More than I have ever wanted anything in my life. But I'll wait until you're ready."

She wiggled around him and a shock of pleasure shot through her. It must have done the same for him, for his elbows buckled slightly and he let out a garbled sound.

"Yes," she gasped. "Please!"

She didn't have to ask him twice. He rolled back and thrust deep inside of her. She lifted to greet him, overcome by the luscious, powerful movement of his body within hers. She gripped him, grinding up and moaning as pleasure tore through her.

He continued, his body rolling over and through her. He dropped his mouth to hers and she opened. They devoured, neither one capable of finesse as mind departed and body became king.

She was shocked by how quickly she was lost, her body moving in a natural rhythm, her mind emptying of everything

Jess Michaels

but the intense pleasure that built with each and every thrust. She shook as he continued that wonderful tempo, drawing her forward, forever forward, forever toward release.

When she found it, it was more powerful than it had ever been before. Pleasure exploded within her, and she cried out. He covered her mouth with his to mute the sound, and she keened against his lips as her fingers dug into his shoulders and her body pulsed out of control with wave after wave of release.

He increased the speed of his thrusts, dragging her relentlessly through sensation. His body tensed, he let out a low growl and then rolled away from her as he came against his hand and flopped back on the pillows beside her.

They lay like that for what felt like a blissful eternity, and then he moved to his side once more and faced her. Concern lined his face, erasing the peace that release had seemed to temporarily grant him.

"Are you well?" he whispered.

She shook her head with a smile. "You worry too much about me, Baldwin. I came to this room wanting exactly what just happened. And if my keening and crying out didn't tell you, I got everything I wanted and more."

He smiled at her description and leaned in to kiss her. She cupped his cheeks and reveled in him. Reveled in the warmth that remained after this powerful joining, reveled in the still tingling pleasure of her body.

That was a gift, and she would cherish it for the rest of her life.

He pulled back and said, "My prerogative is to worry, Helena, and to take care to make everything about this perfect for you. You deserve that. You deserve so much more than I could ever give."

Her heart swelled with those words. Swelled with feelings she had been trying to ignore, trying to combat, since the first moment she'd turned and found this man on the terrace watching her count stars.

But there it was, and it was as undeniable as the physical

draw between them. She loved him. Suddenly and impossibly and powerfully, she loved this man with all that her heart could hold and even more.

She loved him, and she knew that he could never be his. Except for tonight. Except for here.

She cupped the back of his neck and drew him down for another kiss. This one was slower, though, deeper, and he shifted as he began to stroke his hands over her body. She shivered and pulled away.

"Show me," she whispered.

His eyes went wide, but his pupils dilated with renewed desire that matched her own. And as he rolled to cover her once more, she surrendered everything to him.

And knew there was some part of her that she would never get back.

CHAPTER SEVENTEEN

Helena sat in the quiet of a parlor hidden in the back of the house. While the others were napping after yet another day of fun and frolic before they prepared for supper, she was enjoying a book.

Well, enjoying might be too much to say. She was holding a book, she was looking at it. But all she was thinking about was Baldwin and the night before. That sweet, sweet night where he'd made love to her over and over. Pleasure had known no bounds, and she ached from it.

"Oh, Helena, I didn't know you were up and about."

Helena shook her head to clear the thoughts of Baldwin, and rose as Adelaide entered the room. Her blonde hair was done loose, as usual, and she wore a blue gown that matched her eyes perfectly. She was gorgeous, but it wasn't just her pretty face. She had so much confidence.

But Helena knew what Baldwin had said about her. That she had been assaulted, though she was saved before it had gone too far. Somehow Adelaide didn't show the aftereffects.

Helena wondered if Graham helped Adelaide forget, as Baldwin had done for Helena last night.

"Are you well?" Adelaide asked, her face suddenly lining with concern.

"I'm sorry," Helena burst out, cheeks filling with color. "I was just staring at you like a ninny."

"No apologies," Adelaide assured her as she moved forward to catch Helena's free hand. "I interrupted your reading. I can go if you'd like to continue it."

"No," Helena said, setting the book aside. "I would much enjoy your company if you are offering it."

Adelaide smiled and they sat together on the settee. She picked up the book. "Oh, Emma wanted to read this one. She keeps going on about it."

"I'll pass it on to her as soon as I'm finished," Helena vowed. "Perhaps I'll even convince her to write me what she thinks—I'd love to talk to someone about it."

Adelaide set the tome aside and tilted her head to examine Helena more closely. "Do you think it's possible you might see more of Emma, of all of us, once you return to London?"

Helena pursed her lips. "If I am accompanying Charity to events where you are present, of course."

"That isn't what I meant," Adelaide said softly.

Helena got up and paced away. "I don't really belong in your circles, Adelaide, though you're all so kind to include me. We all know the truth of it, don't we? We can't pretend it forever."

"That's poppycock," Adelaide snorted. "And it still isn't what I meant." Helena turned toward her, and Adelaide gave her a look. "I'm asking about you and Baldwin."

Helena's lips parted. "You duchesses are relentless."

Adelaide laughed. "We are that, yes. So if you know that, why don't we stop beating about the bush? What is it between you?"

Helena sighed and returned to her seat. She held Adelaide's gaze evenly and said, "Nothing." Once again Adelaide snorted and Helena threw up her hands. "Very well. More than nothing. We are...we're closer than I ever thought we could be. But it can't happen, Adelaide, no matter what we want."

Adelaide's expression grew troubled. "When you first said that to me, I thought you were being coy. Trying to distance yourself from the kind of feelings so many before you have felt.

But—but it's more than that, isn't it?"

Helena nodded, and relief and disappointment crested through her at once. "It is."

For a moment, Adelaide hesitated. Then she inched closer and reached out to take Helena's hands. The comforting warmth of that touch was a shock to Helena's system, after so long without true friendship to buoy her.

"We are new friends, I know, but I hope good ones. Would you like to talk about it, Helena?" When Helena didn't answer right away, Adelaide sighed. "I know from experience how hard it is to face these sorts of things without a confidante. I did the same when it was Graham and me, and it was trying."

Helena's lips parted. She could not imagine that anything could ever be hard between Northfield and Adelaide. They obviously loved each other deeply. She could also not imagine that her friend hadn't been surrounded by support. But then, she knew so very little about all of the duchesses. There was implied struggle in all their pasts.

"I can't speak to all the reasons that separate Baldwin and me," she said. "Some are not my secrets to tell."

"But if you want to say the ones that are," Adelaide pressed. "I'm a friendly ear who only wants the best for you."

Helena bent her head. "Baldwin said you might…you might understand. You'd been through something similar."

Adelaide leaned closer. "Something similar?"

She lifted her gaze and stared at Adelaide. "I don't want you to think differently of me."

"I couldn't," the duchess assured her gently. "I promise you."

Helena squeezed her eyes shut, and the words began to fall from her lips. Like she had with Baldwin, she told Adelaide all of her past. It was only when she was finished that she looked at the duchess again.

And found her staring back with understanding on her face. "*That* is the scandal," she said softly. "That drove you from Boston."

THE DUKE OF NOTHING

Helena nodded slowly.

Adelaide shook her head. "People are bastards. To blame you for an attack you didn't cause, it makes my stomach turn." Helena drew back from her harsh tone, from the defense she hadn't asked for. Adelaide leaned in. "But my dear, you cannot think that those facts would keep Baldwin from you. You don't think he's the kind of man who would judge that?"

Helena gasped. "Oh, no! No, not at all. He's been nothing but kind and gentle and accepting. He encouraged me to talk to you or to Emma since you two had—"

"Have a similar past." Adelaide squeezed her hand. "Emma and I were very lucky. James stopped her attacker. Graham nearly killed him when he came for me. But yes, we both know a tiny glimpse of the terror you must have felt in those moments."

Helena sucked in a breath, and then she felt the tears begin to fall. She reached up to cover them as shock flowed through her. She had put all this away long ago. And yet having support…it was like she was allowed to remember that she had been hurt. That she had been wronged.

Adelaide clucked her tongue and drew her in for a hard hug. "You cry, love. You just cry all you need to. You've earned that."

Helena relaxed into the embrace, and for a moment she allowed herself the weakness she had fought against for so long. The pain she'd been denied. She sank into it and gave herself the gift of mourning the past, of what she'd lost.

And when she could finally breathe again, Adelaide smiled down at her. "It makes it a bit better, doesn't it? Like a pressure valve that's been released on the heart."

"Yes," Helena agreed through a thick throat. "It does."

Adelaide smoothed a lock of hair away from her face. "But if you say Baldwin doesn't judge you for that, then why do you believe you can't be together?"

Helena straightened up a fraction and sighed. "I can only tell you that my past is not my only failing. I just cannot…be what he needs. It is the way of our world. I must—I must accept it. I must accept it and move forward."

Adelaide's face crumpled just a little. Helena couldn't believe it. This was this woman's empathy for her, her gentle heart that broke for what Helena had endured and would endure.

It meant everything to her to see it.

"I hope you're wrong," Adelaide said at last, and reached out to hug her again. "I truly hope you and Baldwin can find the happiness you so sorely deserve. Life is far too short for anything less."

From behind them, Helena heard someone clear his throat. She and Adelaide turned together, and Helena's heart sank. Her uncle and Charity stood in the doorway to the parlor. Both of them looked annoyed. Angry, even. And she had to steel herself for the consequences of what they'd seen.

"Your Grace," Uncle Peter said, his tone cool.

Adelaide stood, Helena right behind her, and said, "Mr. Shephard, Miss Shephard. Good afternoon."

"You can call me Charity," Charity said, her tone sharp and laced with jealousy that made Helena squeeze her eyes shut.

Adelaide nodded. "Of course. I was just having the loveliest conversation with Helena. You have a gem in her, Mr. Shephard. I hope you appreciate it."

Her uncle's jaw set and he ground out, "Quite. Actually, Charity and I were just talking about our little…gem. Do you think we might have a moment alone with Helena?"

Adelaide turned toward her, one fine eyebrow arching. "If you feel we are finished with our conversation?"

Helena knew the message in her friend's expression, questioning if she would be all right with her family. The truth was, she didn't quite know the answer. But denying them would only make it worse in the long run.

"Perhaps we can continue it later," she suggested gently. "Over supper?"

Adelaide smiled. "I will make sure we are seated next to each other. Perhaps Emma could make a third near us. I would enjoy that very much. I shall go talk to Charlotte and make the arrangements right now."

Helena nodded and Adelaide squeezed her hand before she smiled tightly at Charity and Uncle Peter. She left the room.

The moment she did, Helena's uncle reached behind and shut the door with a loud swish.

"Just what do you think you're doing?" he asked, his rage barely contained. She felt it bubbling below the surface and saw it in the snap of his gaze.

"Doing?" she repeated as she backed up a step from him out of pure instinct.

"We saw you...*hugging* the Duchess of Northfield," Charity spat out. "Completely out of your place."

Helena shook her head. "The duchess was offering a friendly ear," she said. "I did not cross a line."

"Of course you did," her uncle blustered. "You did, and it isn't the first time since our arrival in London that you've done so."

Helena caught her breath. Uncle Peter and Charity didn't know the half of the lines she'd crossed...or did they? She and Baldwin had been careful the night before, but anything was possible.

Charity stepped toward her. "This trip is supposed to be about *me*, Helena! When I suggested you come along, I never thought that you'd ingratiate yourself to the most important people in England. That you'd wheedle your way into their hearts and push me out into the cold."

Helena's lips parted. She heard *hurt* in Charity's tone, not just anger and it set her on her heels. "I never intended to do that. Oh, Charity, my friendships with these people are totally separate from your own. They have no impact on you, I assure you."

"Don't they?" Charity snapped. "Since we came here, and especially since we came out to the Sheffield estate, you have gotten *all* the attention. You've been danced with more than I have, talked to more than I have, consoled more than I have."

Charity's voice caught and she folded her arms. "And—and you shirk your duties, too."

Helena shook her head. "I've been available every time you sought me out."

Charity placed her hands on her hips. "Last night I came looking for you and you weren't in your part of the chamber."

Helena's heart stopped. Oh God, this *was* about Baldwin. They knew. They knew and everything was about to be shattered.

"Charity told me about your absence this afternoon," her uncle said. "And it was the last straw. Where were you?"

"I was not tired," she said carefully. "I didn't want to disturb you by tossing and turning on the settee in the attached room, so I got up to walk around a bit. Hoping it would make me tired."

Charity and Uncle Peter exchanged a look, and then Charity shrugged. "Still," she said. "You are crossing the line."

"You were brought here on the sole balance of my benevolence, girl, don't you forget it. If Charity hadn't insisted and I hadn't agreed, you would have been out on the street in Boston. Your family knew you were a whore who'd worn out whatever purpose you had left. You owe me everything."

Helena flinched, but before she could respond, the door to the parlor opened and Baldwin stepped in. But it wasn't a Baldwin she'd ever seen before. Gone was her gentle lover. Gone was the careful duke.

Standing before her was a raging bull, his face red and his eyes narrowed. And all that anger was focused squarely on her uncle.

Baldwin could hardly breathe as he burst into the parlor and came face-to-face with Helena and her family. What he'd overheard in the hallway, Shephard's sharp and cruel berating, that was bad enough. But coming into the room and seeing

Helena's pale and pained face and the way she was edged up into a corner, trying to make herself as small as possible...

It was enough. He forgot prudence. He forgot propriety. He forgot that she was not his.

He forgot it all and strode into the room in three long strides. "Just what the hell is going on in here?" he growled, pleased he had found enough control to make coherent words.

Shephard jolted in surprise, and Charity took a step back. Helena remained in place, her shoulders still hunched. She glanced at him, her expression a combination of shock and relief and also stark terror.

And he wanted to sweep her up and ride away with her. Ride away from everything that kept them apart. Ride away and never, never come back.

"This is a family matter, Your Grace," Shephard said with another glare for Helena. "I suggest you stay out of it."

"When you are talking to one of my house guests in such a tone in my parlor, I will not stay out of it," Baldwin said. He moved forward a few more steps. "Miss Monroe is a lady, sir. I suggest you keep that in mind."

Somehow he had expected that Shephard would step down at that admonishment. That he would show a little decency. He was to be disappointed. Instead, Shephard leaned in and laughed. "A lady! Is that what Helena has convinced you that she is? Well, let me disabuse you of that notion, Your Grace. My niece is anything but a lady."

Charity gasped and Helena turned her head, her cheeks flush with humiliation. Baldwin lunged forward, and now he was towering over Shephard, ready to swing if need be. Barely containing himself from doing just that.

"Don't test me, Shephard," he said softly.

Shephard was not unaffected. Baldwin swelled with pride at the way the other man trembled ever so slightly. The way a thin sheen of sweat broke out on his upper lip as he stared up into Baldwin's face.

But then something shifted. The fear ebbed, replaced with

a nasty smugness that turned Baldwin's stomach.

"No, boy," the other man said, poking his finger into Baldwin's chest. "Don't you test me."

They held their stare for a moment, for too long. Then Baldwin pointed to the door. "Get out of this room, sir. Or I shall have you removed."

Shephard chuckled as he motioned to Charity. "Come along, dear. And you, Helena."

"She stays," Baldwin snapped. "There is no way she will go anywhere with you until you think about your behavior toward her."

Shephard sent her a nasty look, then caught Charity's arm and all but dragged her from the room, leaving Baldwin alone with Helena.

He spun on her, but she was not looking at him with gratitude. She didn't look happy at what he'd done. She was shaking her head, over and over, and her face was pale and sick.

"Helena," he said softly.

She caught her breath on a sob and said, "You shouldn't have done that, Baldwin."

CHAPTER EIGHTEEN

Baldwin stared at Helena, and she could see he was surprised that she hadn't launched herself into his arms and declared him her hero. Perhaps part of her wanted to do that. There was a moment when her bully of an uncle had actually looked afraid, and there was no denying that she had enjoyed that far more than she should have.

But it didn't change the facts of the situation she found herself in. And that moment of pleasure, just like all the moments of pleasure she'd stolen lately, would have dire consequences in the end.

Baldwin's jaw set as he marched across the room and gently shut the door, giving them privacy that they ought not have. And yet she had no energy left to argue that fact.

"He attacked you, Helena. You could not truly expect me to stand by and allow it."

She threw up her hands. "Why not? As he said, it was a family quarrel."

His hands moved to his hips and the same stern and angry expression he'd had earlier returned to his handsome face. "Well, then I shall respond to you the same way I did to him. He was berating you in my home, under my roof. I would intervene for any guest who was treated in such a manner."

He edged closer, and suddenly she was very aware of him. Very aware of the look in his eyes. The one that said he wanted to touch her.

"Baldwin," she whispered.

He ignored the warning in her tone. "And the answer I did not give to him but will to you is that I certainly would not stand by while *you* were berated. *You*, Helena, a woman I know intimately. A woman I care for. A woman who is worth ten Peter Shephards."

She shook her head. "If I were worth ten Peter Shephards, we would be having a different conversation," she whispered. "But I'm not. And while I appreciate your motives, you must see that confronting him could very well make it worse for me. I know it will. And he might even hurt you. He all but outwardly threatened you."

He shook his head, and then he reached out and caught her arms, drawing her forward, until she was pressed against him, staring up at him. His body heat wrapped around her, his muscles supported her, and he became the only thing that mattered in this room. In this world.

"Has no one *ever* stood up for you?" he asked, his voice cracking.

Tears stung her eyes, and she blinked in vain to try to clear them. She had no idea what to say to him. How to make him understand. How to make him see that what he was doing was fruitless.

Finally she choked out, "I'm not yours."

His expression darkened, filled with a pain she didn't want to analyze. She thought he might pull away, but instead he bent his head and suddenly his lips were on hers.

She had no ability to resist when he touched her. Reason departed, prudence did not exist. All that mattered was how sweetly he kissed her—and then not as sweetly, and then not sweetly at all. Passion rose between them and she lost herself in it, letting it wash away everything else she had felt in the past hour.

He tugged her closer, backing her against the nearest wall, dragging his mouth away from hers, to her neck as he pushed against her with animal drive and undeniable desire. She wanted him so much, consequences be damned. Her body screamed at her to open to him, to surrender to him. To give and give and give until he overwhelmed her with pleasure that made the future seem bright.

Perhaps she would have at that. Perhaps he would have lost himself and she would have given him the path to find her. But before things could go that far the door beside them opened, and before they could part from the compromised position they were in, the Duke of Tyndale strode in.

"Baldwin, Charlotte told me that—"

Helena shoved at Baldwin's chest with all her might and staggered away from him, but she felt Tyndale's gaze on her and her cheeks flamed with humiliated fire as she did everything she could not to look at him.

"I'm so sorry," Tyndale said, having the decency, at least, to glance away. "I did not realize you were here, Miss Monroe."

She shook her head and moved around Baldwin toward the door. "I must go. I must go anyway."

She tripped on the edge of the carpet in her haste, and Matthew caught her elbow and gently steadied her. "Miss Monroe—"

"Helena—" Baldwin said at the same time.

She waved her hand. "Please don't. Please don't!"

Then she ran from the room, her body shaking and her eyes filling with tears as the ramifications of everything that had happened in that room filled her with heartbreak and fear.

"Well timed," Baldwin snapped at Matthew as he watched Helena flee the room like the hounds of hell itself were on her heels. The expression on her face was burned into his mind: a combination of humiliation and heartbreak, desire and regret. He had caused her all this pain and he hated himself for it.

Matthew stared at him wordlessly and then shut the door. He leaned back against it, arms folded, and said, "This is enough. Tell me what the hell is going on, Baldwin. You and Helena are obviously...involved."

"Obviously," Baldwin snorted as he strode over to the sideboard and poured himself a tall glass of scotch. Matthew waved off when he offered him the same. "I'd be stupid to deny it when you walked in on us in such an entanglement."

There was a sudden flash of hope on Matthew's face as he pushed off the door and took a step toward Baldwin. "Does this mean you've chosen your bride?"

Baldwin took a long swig of the liquor and shook his head. "No," he whispered.

Tyndale's expression grew hard and dark. "I would expect this kind of behavior out of...Robert, perhaps. But *you*? She's a lady, Baldwin! How dare you make sport of her virtue?"

Baldwin slammed the drink down. "First, don't compare me to Roseford. You know how I feel about his whoring."

"I do, you make it clear that you don't approve of how he drowns himself in sex. But it sounds like you aren't far behind."

Baldwin shook his head. "I'm not making fucking sport of her, I assure you. If I had any other choice, I would—" He cut himself off because if he said it out loud, he'd buckle beneath it.

Tyndale stared at him. "You *can't* marry her."

Baldwin paced away. "No."

"Why? And don't fucking change the subject or lie to me. I've had enough of it."

Baldwin pivoted. He and Matthew and Ewan had all been very close as boys. The cousins had accepted him like their long-lost brother, and he'd counted on them so many times during the years, outside of their relationship in their club.

And now he looked at Matthew and all he wanted to do was confess. The desire pulsed up inside of him, hard to ignore thanks to the raw emotion that snapped through him.

"Please," Matthew said, softer and gentler. "Let me help you."

Baldwin bent his head. There was no denying this anymore. He had to tell Matthew the truth. And so…he did.

The words poured from him, an explanation of bad debts and worse decisions, of his father's failings and his own. Of the missing parts of his ledger, the debts that had been purchased behind his back and the fear that accompanied all those awful facts.

He talked for half an hour and Matthew said nothing. He just stared, wide-eyed, until Baldwin collapsed into the nearest chair, spent from confession and heavy with fear at what his friend's reaction would be.

"And now you know it all."

Matthew got up and poured the drink he had refused at the beginning. He drank half of it before he said, "Am I the only one?"

Baldwin cleared his throat. "No. She knows."

"She." Matthew arched a brow. "Helena."

Baldwin nodded slowly. "I had to…explain why I couldn't pursue her."

Matthew shut his eyes. "I see. And what did she say?"

He scrubbed a hand over his face. "She's so bloody accustomed to being treated no better than a dog that she accepted it. She *claims* to understand it. It's even how we ended up in the position that I would be kissing her in the parlor."

"So you'll kiss her and do…whatever else you've done," Matthew said, his voice low and angry. Baldwin flinched. "But you will not marry her."

"I *can't*. I know you must judge me for all my mistakes."

"No, not for your mistakes," Matthew snapped. "Anyone could have gone down the path you did. I can totally understand how you might have come to this point. What I judge you for is loving this woman, for it is obvious that you do love her, and that you would walk away from that like it's nothing."

Baldwin got up and moved on him. "Trust me, it is not nothing. It's—"

He broke off and tried to turn away, but Matthew caught his

arm and wrenched him back in place. "What is it?"

"Complicated," Baldwin said softly.

Matthew released him, horror passing over his features. He backed away, step by step, and stared at Baldwin like he had never seen him before. The expression made Baldwin's heart hurt.

"*Complicated*," Matthew repeated, his voice empty. "No, *complicated* is having the woman you loved buried in the ground because of something you did. *Complicated* is watching her die and not being able to do anything about it. *Complicated* is having your future taken from you and yet everyone expects you to move on like it never existed. *That* is complicated. What you're doing? That's not complicated. It's cowardly."

Baldwin ducked his head. He had no response, after all. Matthew wasn't wrong.

"I'm sorry."

Matthew shrugged. "Right now you certainly are. So you'll just walk away then. Let her go."

"I must, even though I fear what will happen when she's no longer under my protection."

Matthew's eyes narrowed. "Why?"

"Her uncle is…cruel. Hateful. I don't know if he's hurt her, I do think he might be capable of it." Baldwin clenched his fists as he thought of how enraged Shephard had been at Helena when he intervened.

"Even better," Matthew muttered. "Well, how about this? I'll marry her."

Baldwin jerked his gaze to Matthew. Tyndale was standing, his arms folded across his chest, staring at Baldwin with…challenge to his gaze.

"Don't even joke," Baldwin said.

Matthew arched a brow. "You think I am? Everyone expects me to marry. I like Helena well enough, and it sounds like she needs to be saved. Since you will not do anything, that's the perfect solution for everyone. Isn't it?"

Baldwin sagged. What Tyndale was offering was exactly

what Helena needed. Matthew had money and standing. He would protect her. And yet the idea of having to see her all the time, watching Matthew hold claim over her. Watching them come to care for each other, for he had no doubt Helena could melt even Matthew's damaged heart over time...

"The very idea kills me," he admitted. "It would be like ripping my own heart out and letting you destroy it."

Matthew's expression softened. "Because you love her."

Baldwin nodded this time, finally allowing himself to express what he'd been trying to deny for days. And it hurt just as much as he'd feared it would. He loved Helena. He wanted her.

And he still didn't see a way out.

"If you love her, *do* something about it," Matthew said. "There's still time. Forget the rest. Your heart is telling you what to do, isn't it?"

Baldwin shuddered. "If I did this, if I married her, I would be walking away from my duties. The debts wouldn't be paid. The truth would come out. It would destroy my family."

"Love is worth any sacrifice," Matthew said. "If you don't do it, you will spend your life wishing you had. The rest will work itself out."

Shutting his eyes, Baldwin draped his arms over his knees and drew in a long breath. Matthew was offering him a lifeline. Imperfect, yes, with so much destruction as a consequence.

And now he had to decide if he would take that chance, and those consequences. He had to decide now.

Helena's entire body shook as she staggered into the chamber she'd been sharing with Charity. She somehow made her way to the settee and dropped down on it, flopping an arm over her face as she tried to calm her ragged breathing and slow her racing heart.

This afternoon had been an utter travesty. Not only had the confrontation between Baldwin and her uncle very likely made everything worse for her, but to have the Duke of Tyndale walk in while Baldwin had her pinned to the wall? With him grinding up against her, her surrendering like a wanton?

She had no idea what would come of that. She liked Tyndale, of course. She felt he was a kind person. Perhaps he wouldn't talk to anyone else about the scene. But she couldn't be certain.

"And now she's having a lay about."

Helena jerked to a seated position and turned to watch her uncle and cousin enter the chamber. Charity's head was bent, but Uncle Peter looked smug as usual. He arched a brow at her.

"You understand something, little miss. You are going back to Boston as soon as I can book you passage."

Helena's stomach turned, but she somehow managed to keep her expression calm as she stared up at him. In the end, Boston was likely the best option for her, not that she'd ever thought she'd say that. She had no one there. Her family had abandoned her. But that was better than staying here, being treated so cruelly and eventually watching Baldwin marry some heiress.

"I'm going to go get a drink," her uncle said, and left the room without a backward glance for either his daughter or his niece.

When he had gone, Helena forced herself to get up. Charity was watching her now, her blue eyes unreadable. Helena smoothed her dress and wished she could smooth her emotions so easily. "Why do you hate me so much?" she asked.

Charity flinched, and to Helena's surprise, a look of hurt crossed her face. "I-I don't," she said.

Helena stared at her in utter disbelief. Finally, she motioned her head toward the door. "Well, *he* does. But don't worry, Charity, it seems that you'll get your wish. I'll be gone soon and then no one will come close to dulling your shine. Excuse me, I need a walk."

She turned on her heel and left the room. She heard Charity say her name, but didn't look back. She just kept walking.

CHAPTER NINETEEN

Baldwin paced the parlor in long strides, only hesitating when he pivoted back to walk the opposite way. All the while, his brain turned. It had been less than twenty-four hours since his brutal conversation with Matthew, but those hours had seemed like an eternity.

That feeling was made worse by the fact that Helena had not come down for supper the night before, nor for games afterward. Her uncle had looked very smug when he claimed she had a headache. Baldwin's only comfort was that the servants who had taken a tray up to her had told him that she was well, not hurt. Just…hiding. Or imprisoned, like a princess in a tower.

Instead of riding to her rescue, Baldwin had spent a long night in his study. He'd gone over every ledger, every contingency, weighing each option as he tied himself in knots. He'd not come to a decision until he'd entered his chamber and felt a crushing disappointment that Helena hadn't been there waiting for him again.

And so…here he was. With one thing left to do before he took the future in front of him with both hands. There would be consequences to that future.

His mother and Charlotte stepped into the parlor, with Ewan behind them. The two women were laughing and Ewan's grin was wide. Baldwin took a moment to examine their happy faces. These were people he loved. He'd done so much to hurt them.

He'd done so much to try to ensure he would never hurt them again.

Now he was going to hurt them all with the truth. And pray they could forgive him.

"Oh, Baldwin," Charlotte said, her smile falling as she looked at him. "Oh, dearest, what is it?"

As his sister rushed across the room to hug him, Ewan closed the door, his gaze narrowing, his expressive face filled with support and love. Their mother stared at him, too, the color gone from her cheeks. She was the only one who had even an inkling of their troubles.

She was about to have more. He hoped she wouldn't be crushed under the weight of it like he'd been all this time.

"I'm fine," Baldwin said softly as he squeezed Charlotte's hands in an attempt to reassure her. "Thank you all for coming to join me so early in the day."

"What is it?" his mother asked, her voice shaking. "Something has happened?"

He held her stare, and in it he saw all her fear, all her strength. "Mama, it's time they know the truth."

The duchess buckled slightly and Ewan rushed forward to catch her elbow. Gently, he guided her to a settee and helped her take her place.

"Must you?" she whispered when she'd gathered herself. "Oh, Baldwin, *must* you?"

Charlotte stared back and forth between her mother and brother. Her sharp gaze was confused and anxious. "What is going on? What is the truth?"

Baldwin took her hand and took her to sit beside their mother. Ewan stood behind then, resting a hand on Charlotte's shoulder. She reached up to cover it, and Baldwin found himself staring at the couple for a moment. This was love. This was support. This was everything.

"You've asked me numerous times in the past few years about my change in…mood," he began. "Both you and Ewan have been concerned."

The pair nodded together.

"Baldwin," his mother whispered.

"It's all right, Mama," he reassured her. "They have a right to know and—and so do you, for you have been kept in the dark, as well."

She tilted her head. "There's more?"

Charlotte pursed her lips. "Will someone *please* explain what's going on?"

Baldwin drew a deep breath. There was truly no way to do this except for quickly and efficiently. "The Sheffield entail is nearly devoid of all funds. There is almost nothing but the land."

As their mother put her head in her hands with a soft sob, Charlotte stared at him, mouth dropped open. Ewan came around to stand beside the settee. He made a few hand signs and Charlotte forced herself to look at him.

"He—he's asking you to clarify. There is *nothing* left?" She shook her head. "How is that possible, Baldwin? Did something happen? We never wanted for anything."

Baldwin nodded slowly. "I know. Father kept his secrets very well. Mama and I knew nothing of the situation until I inherited and the ledgers were revealed. He was constantly robbing Peter to pay Paul. He had debts all over the countryside."

"How?" Charlotte whispered.

Baldwin flinched at the pained tone to her voice. He was crushing her illusions about her father. A man she had adored. He knew how she felt. He'd experienced the same thing.

"He had a compulsion," Baldwin said softly. "To gamble. I saw it firsthand, though I didn't know the consequences until it was far too late."

"That is why you've been so dark, so dour, since you inherited,'" Charlotte translated as Ewan signed. "Why didn't you talk to us? To your family or your friends?"

Baldwin bent his head. "Because I made it worse and I didn't want you to judge me."

His mother lifted her gaze and held his. "What?"

173

His cheeks grew heated. These were the parts she had never known. The parts he'd kept from her to protect himself. Now he forced himself to explain about his own bad choices. How he'd dug them in even further.

"I am humiliated," he said when it was all out and the room had been silent for too long as his family digested his confession. "I didn't want you to know."

Charlotte had been staring at him as he spoke, but now she stood slowly. He watched, wary, as she moved toward him. Then she wrapped her arms around him and hugged him just as tightly as she ever had. Her voice trembled as she whispered, "How horrible that you felt you had to carry this burden alone. Oh, Baldwin, I'm so sorry."

He drew back. "You're sorry? I'm the one who has disillusioned you about our father and destroyed our family name."

She shook her head. "I am disillusioned, of course. But that isn't your doing—it's his. He had many good qualities. Right now I am stunned, but this news doesn't change how kind he could be. How supportive. How loving."

Baldwin's brow wrinkled. He'd been dealing with the fallout of his father's bad behavior for so long that he hadn't been able to recall those things that Charlotte said. Now they flooded back. His father teaching him to ride. His father praising him for successes and comforting him in his failures.

He swayed a little as those loving feelings returned. His sister's gift to him.

"There's more, I'm afraid," he croaked out as he motioned Charlotte back to her seat.

His mother moaned anew. "Oh no."

He nodded. "I'm sorry. There were three outstanding debts that I could not trace the source of. While we've been here, my solicitor has sent word that they've been bought by one private party."

Ewan shook his head and signed as Charlotte translated, "Bought? Someone bought all three debts? Why?"

"I have no idea," Baldwin said, holding Ewan's stare and watching his friend's face twist in horror at the possibilities.

"There can be no good reason," Charlotte whispered.

Ewan signed, "How much?"

Baldwin shot his mother a side glance before he said, "Five thousand pounds."

The duchess leapt to her feet, covering her mouth with both hands. Charlotte simply stared at him, and Ewan looked sick.

Baldwin let them process the terrible news for a moment, then drew a deep breath. "There's a reason I'm telling you all of this at last, when I've kept it a secret for so long. And it is this…I'm in love with Helena Monroe."

His mother lowered her hands slowly. "Oh, Baldwin."

"Mama and I had created a list of suitable heiresses with large enough fortunes to help get us out of a portion of this mess father and I created, but…I love her. And she has nothing," Baldwin said, and there was a huge weight that lifted from his shoulders when he got to say those words. The last secret was out. He was no longer alone in bearing it all.

Charlotte's eyes had filled with tears and she reached for Ewan's hand. "Baldwin…oh, this should be such happy news. We adore Helena, and anyone can see the connection between you."

"Loving her is the best thing I've ever done in my life," he whispered. "If the circumstances were any different, I would offer for her without hesitation. But the circumstances are not different. So when I offer for her, it will cause farther-reaching consequences. I knew you had to understand them, to voice your objections. You have that right."

"You're offering for her," his mother whispered.

He nodded immediately, for he felt no hesitation in the decision he had made. "I am. I must. A life lived without her is…unfathomable. I spent the night going over figures, reading over the ledgers, trying to find a way to make it work. It will require whittling down to almost nothing. The art will be sold, some of the furnishings in the other three houses. The London home will be where we stay almost all the time." He shook his head. "I'll tell her, of course, that it will be an austere life."

"And what about these debts you spoke of," Charlotte whispered. "Does it take into account if those are called back by this mysterious buyer?"

He hesitated. "That is the sticking point. I have no idea of the terms that will be laid out by this mysterious person. I can't plan for them. So…no. If the debts are called in, then—then the worst may still happen."

Ewan signed something. A few simple slashes of his fingers in the air, but Charlotte's expression crumpled as she stared at him.

"I love you," she whispered.

Ewan smiled down at her, his reply clear on his face. The words were not needed.

"He says he will pay the debt," she said, rising to take his hand.

Baldwin's lips parted. "It's five thousand pounds. A small fortune."

Ewan stared at him a moment, then reached into his pocket and withdrew a small silver notebook. He scribbled on it and handed it over.

"'Luckily I have a large fortune,'" Baldwin read softly. "'I insist.'"

He handed the notebook back and dropped his head. "I've become a charity case for my family and friends."

Ewan caught his arm, and when Baldwin looked up, Ewan was shaking his head. He signed furiously as Charlotte translated. "Never! This is not charity. It is a gift, just as this family has been the greatest gift of my life."

"Ewan," the Duchess of Sheffield breathed. "That you would do this for my son…"

Ewan continued to sign without breaking his gaze from Baldwin. Charlotte's voice was thick as she translated, "My brother."

Baldwin nodded. Oh yes, Ewan had been his brother long

before his marriage to Charlotte. And now he offered the lifeline in this storm. Would it be easy? No. Never. But now he had a chance at survival.

"I accept your generous offer. If the worst happens, I will do everything in my power to repay it, though I know there is no way I can truly offer recompense for your kindness, nor the wonderful life you've given my sister," Baldwin said as he reached out to embrace Ewan. "You don't know how much it means."

When they parted, he turned back to find his sister and mother standing together, their arms around each other. Both had eyes sparkling with tears. He could see Charlotte's approval in what he was about to do. It really came down to their mother.

"Mama," he said softly, coming forward to take her hands as Charlotte stepped away. "In the end, this is your name as well as mine that will be on the line. I cannot promise that Father's sins will not still come out. That there won't be a scandal."

She stared at him a long moment, then over to Charlotte and Ewan. "I have only ever wanted your happiness, my two loves. I can see that if I denied you the chance to marry Helena, I would watch you live a life of misery. That would be far worse a consequence, I think, than having my friends whisper that my husband was a debtor. Half of their husbands are no better. If this is what you need to be happy, I will support it with a full heart and at full voice to anyone who questions it."

Relief washed through Baldwin, and he lifted both her hands up and kissed each one in turn. "Thank you, Mama."

"It sounds like you have someone to go talk to," Charlotte said, her laughter filling the room like music. "Go do it quickly. I would love to celebrate with our friends before this country party ends."

Baldwin looked at them, his family, his everything. He'd spent years trying to protect them, trying to protect himself. Fearing the worst-case scenario that they would blame or reject him for the things he'd done.

Now that seemed like such an empty fear, because of course

they would love and accept him. He'd been so wrong to expect anything less of them.

"Thank you," he said. "And yes, I think it's time to see if any of this matters and talk to Helena."

Ewan waved him out of the room while his mother and sister beamed after him. And as he strode down the hall toward his study to gather himself and plan what he would say to the love of his life, for the first time in years he felt happy. He felt free.

He could only hope that what he offered would be enough for Helena. Because what mattered in that moment was giving her everything he could, and praying that she would take it, and him. Flaws and all.

CHAPTER TWENTY

Helena stood at the window beside the settee she'd called a bed and sighed as rain streaked down the glass. It was a fitting thing, the storm. It matched the rioting emotions in her own heart. She rested her head back and shut her eyes with a shiver.

How had things come so far from a night counting stars on the terrace to…this? With a guillotine hanging over her head and her future so uncertain? Not that she'd change a thing. She'd had those stolen moments with Baldwin, and they meant the world to her.

There was a light knock on the chamber door behind her and Helena stiffened. After the past twenty-four hours, she wasn't equipped to deal with any more drama. Not that drama normally knocked so gently.

She moved to the door and opened it, and was surprised to find Walker standing there. The butler smiled. "I'm sorry to trouble you, miss, but His Grace has requested that you join him in his study, if you are not otherwise occupied at the moment."

Her heart throbbed as she tried, and failed, to read Walker's expression. "His Grace wants to—to see me," she said.

He nodded. "At your earliest convenience. Do you have a message to return to him?"

"I will join him momentarily." Her voice shook, and she blushed, for it was very noticeable.

Walker inclined his head. "Very good, miss. And you know

where the study is?"

"Yes," Helena whispered as she thought of the night she had shared with Baldwin there. The butler smiled again and then slipped away.

She stood staring into the empty hall for a moment, then shook off her surprise. She had no idea why Baldwin would call her to him. It was ten in the morning, early by the standards of many. Her cousin was still abed, after all.

After their last encounter, he could want to say anything to her. He might want to check on her. Or perhaps he wanted to tell her that Tyndale disapproved of what he'd walked in on the previous day. He might even want to end their affair.

"Oh, do just go down," she snapped out loud to herself. "Standing up here and running over the possibilities is no help."

She moved to the mirror and quickly checked herself. Aside from looking like she'd had no sleep, which she hadn't, she was presentable. She drew a deep breath, and marched out of the room and down the stairs. As she meandered through the hallways, she tried to stay calm and finally resorted to counting the number of doors that were between her and her fate.

At last she reached Baldwin's office door. It was open a crack and she quietly stepped inside. He was standing at his window, his hands clasped behind him. She drank in the sight of him for the briefest of moments. He was so handsome. So strong. For just a flash of time, he'd been hers.

Letting him go was going to be crushing.

She shook away the last thought and cleared her throat to draw his attention.

He turned, and she caught her breath a second time, though for a far different reason. Baldwin's face was filled with…light. She'd never seen him thus, and it shocked her. He always had a sense of melancholy around him, responsibility that was drowning him every day.

Now it was different. It was as if he had been brought to life. She couldn't help but step toward him and that light, to feel healed by it and lifted by it.

"Helena," he said, crossing the room to her. "Thank you for coming."

She jerked out a nod. "I...of course, Baldwin. Of course. Has something happened?"

He tilted his head and examined her face with another of those little smiles that were so lovely to see. "Why would you think something has happened?"

She drew in a shaky breath. "You're changed. I don't know, there is something different in the air around you."

He laughed as he moved to shut the door and gave them the privacy she so longed for. The privacy they likely shouldn't have. But she ignored that.

She wanted to be alone with him. She had no idea how many times she would get to do so. There were only two days left at his house party. Perhaps a week or two before she'd be shuttled back to America.

She pushed the thought away as he returned and caught her hand, drawing her to the settee and taking a place there beside her. Too close.

"Leave it to you to recognize even the most subtle of shifts in me," he said, reaching out to trace a finger down her cheek.

She swallowed hard and tried not to lean in to the gentle warmth of his touch. "*Has* something happened?"

He nodded, and his expression grew more serious. Not melancholy, just serious. "It has, Helena. Not all at once, but in little increments. Little shifts over time that take a man from a certain place to another in a way that he hardly notices, before one day he wakes up and he's...here. With you."

"I-I don't understand," she whispered.

"I know you don't. I'm going to explain." He shook his head with a small laugh. "I'm actually quite nervous, though, so I hope you will be gentle with me."

She drew back. "You? Nervous. I can hardly picture that."

"You do that to me," he said. "You always have. I should have known that first night."

Her hands had begun to shake and she gripped them in her

lap as she stared into his face and saw all her hopes and dreams reflected there. Only they couldn't be. "What should you have known?"

He leaned in closer, holding her stare with his. Never letting her look away. He smiled once more. "I love you, Helena Monroe."

She froze. This was a dream. There was no other explanation for Baldwin sitting across from her, telling her he loved her. Except when she pinched herself, she didn't wake.

"Please don't," she said, jumping up to distance herself from him. "Please don't say that to me."

Baldwin watched as Helena staggered across the room, holding her hands up to ward him away. She did not look happy at his confession—she looked horrified.

Slowly he got to his feet and smoothed his jacket. "Not the reaction I was hoping for, I admit," he said, trying to keep his tone calm. "Do you not care for me?"

He braced himself for the answer, though there was no bracing for her rejection. Just the thought of it made his stomach turn.

She shook her head over and over. "You know I do," she said at last, her breath short, her words trembling. "But it's cruel to tell me this when we both know the situation. I've accepted that we can't be together. Please don't make me say those words out loud. I will drown in them."

His relief nearly buckled him. She didn't know his decision yet. She didn't know his offer. Her fear kept her from him, not a lack of feeling.

He stepped forward. "Say the words," he encouraged. "I will not let you drown."

Her face crumpled. "Please."

"Say them," he repeated.

"I love you," she whispered, ducking her head. "I have loved you from the first moment I met you. But we both know I have nothing to offer you."

He frowned at how easily she accepted that she would lose. That was the place she had been placed for so long. By her family and friends…by him. When they were married, he would help her with that. He knew she could find her confidence. Emma had, after all, and she had been very similar to Helena when she and James first wed.

"You have yourself," he said softly as he tucked a finger beneath her chin and made her look up at him. Tears sparkled in her eyes, and they broke his heart. "You are worth more than gold."

"I am not," she said. "And that isn't what we're talking about."

"No, we're talking about money," he said with a sigh. "A topic that should never have to be mixed with love."

"But it is!" she burst out, stepping away from him. "I know your position, Baldwin. I have accepted it as best I can. Please don't rip my soul to shreds like this. I can hardly bear it."

"Helena, listen to me." He caught her hands so she couldn't pull away, and she instantly stopped trying. She stared up at him and the first tear began to fall. She had been so strong, so good when it came to what he could and couldn't do for her.

Now he saw how much of a struggle that had been. How cruel it had been to her. He hated himself for making her suffer even for one moment.

"Matthew offered to marry you," he said.

She jerked back, her eyes going wide. "What?"

"I explained everything to him after yesterday after he saw us together in the parlor. Everything about my financial situation, about you and the cruelty your uncle's has shown to you. I told him why I couldn't be with you, despite my feelings, and he rightly called me out for what I am: a coward. He offered to marry you and save you from what your uncle could do—will do, if left to his own devices."

Her breath was so short now he feared she would collapse. "I-I don't understand. Tyndale would marry me?"

He nodded, and his stomach churned with even the memory of that moment. "Yes. When he made that offer my entire world shattered. I knew it would solve your problems. That it would allow me to see you safe. But it killed me to think of it. And I knew, without a doubt, that I could not live in a world where you weren't mine."

Her lips parted in shock. "Baldwin..." His name was a whisper on her lips, barely audible.

He continued, "I've kept the secret of my father's bad behavior, and my own, for years. But for you I've told my family."

She drew away. "You told your family?"

"Everything. Ewan has offered to help. And if he does, then there is some hope for me. I cannot promise you the life that Tyndale would. He has funds, he could make you a princess if you wanted to be treated as such. You deserve that. But the life that I will promise you is filled with love, Helena. I will not lie and say it wouldn't be a struggle. It would be austere. There may be scandal if some of those debts are revealed. But I love you."

"You are offering me a future?" she asked. "Baldwin, that is throwing away everything you could have! Many of the prospects would help get you out of the situation entirely. You could rebuild, you could—"

"I want you." He cupped her cheeks gently. "I love you, Helena. And that has come to matter far more than anything else in this world. I love you and I want to marry you."

She was blinking. Just blinking. Like she didn't understand. Like she couldn't.

"You would give up everything for me?" she whispered.

He drew back, for he had long ceased to think of marrying her as giving anything up. It would be gaining everything. And yet she still didn't understand that. "I would walk across the sun for you," he said. "I would swim across the sea. I would give up my title, my name, any small thing I had left. I would die for you, Helena Monroe. And I will live for you if you just stop looking at me like I've gone mad and tell me that you'll be mine. My wife. For the rest of my days, be they short or long. Please, please say you'll marry me."

She was trembling now, her façade cracking. "And what if you come to regret it?" she asked.

He shook his head. "I never could. Don't you understand? You are the only person in this world who I can be who I am, truly who I am, around. You lighten my every load, how could I ever regret that? Please. Please, Helena."

Her breath drew in on a sob, and she nodded. "Yes. Yes, I love you, and the idea of being away from you, of being alone without you, has broken me into so many pieces. If you are sure, then yes. I will marry you, Baldwin."

The joy that flooded him was so powerful and so foreign that he nearly buckled under it. He drew her in and kissed her, his fingers smoothing over her cheeks as he tasted her tears, tasted his own. She wrapped her arms around his neck and lifted against him, flattening her body to his like she feared she would lose him. That this was a dream or a fantasy.

And it was. Just one that they would get to live out together forever. In that moment, he fully put aside his worries and surrendered to the gentle passion of her kiss. To the realization that she would be his now. Forever.

He leaned in, laying her back against the settee. She shifted and he lowered himself over her, loving the feel of the length of her body beneath his. No one in his life had ever stoked this kind of passion in him. This need to claim and have and love forever.

He could think of no better way to celebrate their engagement than this. To make love to her without the barriers that had been between them the last time.

She must have read his mind, because of course she could read his mind. She pulled away slightly. "We won't be…interrupted?"

He smiled. "No. It's early still and I locked the door."

"You did?" She laughed. "I was so caught up I didn't

notice."

"I was crafty," he said, brushing his lips against hers. "I'll find my ways when it comes to being alone with you."

"I suppose we have the rest of our lives to figure out how to be crafty together," she said, and her face was lit up with the same wonder that he felt on his own.

They were going to be together. Forever. He grinned as he covered her mouth again. But the playfulness quickly faded as desire rose in him. She gave so completely, so openly. Despite her past, Helena had not lost her sweetness or her passion. He had never been so glad of anything.

He began to rock against her as his hands roved down her side, then across to gently squeeze her breast. She let out a sound of pleasure and her hips nudged his, sending a jolt of awareness and sensation up his already hard cock.

"The things you do to me," he murmured as he slid his mouth from hers to her neck.

"Show me," she whispered, her voice shaking in the quiet of the room.

He lifted his head and caught her hand, drawing it between them and pressing it to his cock. She groaned as she touched him, cupped him, began to stroke him through the suddenly too-heavy fabric of his trousers.

"I need you," he grunted.

She nodded, and her hand slid to unbutton the front placard of his trousers. As she did so, he pushed her skirts up, bunching around her hips. She parted her legs and he settled between them, his heat finding hers. His cock sliding home as she gasped out his name in pleasure.

He couldn't be so verbose. When her tight, slick heat pulsed around him, he lost all ability to think, let alone form coherent words. He was animal in that moment, lost in the sensations of pleasure that ordered him to take. To claim. To make his in the most permanent way he could imagine.

He thrust, short and hard, and her fingers tightened against his back. He watched her face as he took her. Her mouth parted with pleasure, her eyes fluttered shut. He memorized every twitch and moan, guiding his motions through her reactions. He watched her build to orgasm and he loved every moment of that journey as they slowly took it together.

At last her eyes flew open and went wide. She let out a garbled cry and her sheath began to pulse around him, milking him with her pleasure, demanding he merge it with his own. And he did, thrusting harder through her crisis, reveling in the way his balls tightened. Electric sensation shot through him. He slammed his mouth to hers, letting his cries of pleasure be lost against her lips as he pumped hard and hot into her clenching body.

He collapsed against her, pressing kisses to her neck as she smoothed her hands over his back. She was his. Truly his in a way he hadn't allowed before. A way that ensured there would be no going back, not that he wanted to do so.

Because she was the love of his life, and he couldn't wait to tell the world.

"That was wonderful," she murmured, pressing her mouth to his neck. "Every time is wonderful. I never imagined it could be like that."

He rolled a little, balancing precariously on the edge of the settee so he could face her. Their bodies parted with the motion, and she let out a little sigh of displeasure that made him smile. "Just think of how wonderful it will be when we aren't sneaking around. Or fraught with danger and potential loss."

She slid her fingers into his hair, massaging his scalp gently. "I might miss fraught with danger," she said with a laugh.

He arched a brow. "Noted, Miss Monroe. I can certainly make sure there is a little after we're married. I'll make love to you by lakes and in side rooms at parties if the fear of being caught makes you mewl my name so prettily."

Dark pink color filled her cheeks. But there was also a little interest in her eyes at the idea, and he chuckled. He would definitely file this information away.

"Now, I would very much like to exploit the potential

danger the study puts us in. However…" He sat up and drew her up with him. They shifted around, putting clothes back in place. She laughed as she smoothed down his hair and he tucked her errant curls back into place. Soon they both looked somewhat more reasonable.

"We have one unpleasantness we must face, I'm afraid," he said at last.

Her expression twisted and she snuggled a little closer to him. "My uncle."

He nodded. "Your uncle. I want you to understand I'm not going to ask him for your hand. I'm telling him I'm taking it. It's a courtesy he isn't owed."

Her lips pursed and he could see all her anxiety return. How he hated it. He hoped someday she would no longer feel any of it.

"When you do this," she said, her voice shaky, "just be prepared. He is entirely awful, especially when crossed. He may not be able to threaten you with a return to Boston as he did me, but he'll do anything in his power to make this as terrible as he can."

Baldwin jolted. "He threatened to send you to America?"

She nodded slowly. "A promise, really, more than a threat."

The rage he'd felt before, when he'd come upon Peter Shephard berating her in the parlor, lifted again. Only this time he had more tools to protect her.

"I will never let him hurt you again," he said softly.

She smiled, and it lit up his world in endless color. In that moment, he realized this was how his life would be from now on. The difficulties made easier by this woman's enormous heart, by the light she carried with her so effortlessly.

He leaned in to kiss her and then stood, drawing her with him. "Come, let's get this over with, and then we can do nothing but celebrate."

He could see her lingering hesitation, but she nodded nonetheless and allowed him to lead her to the door.

CHAPTER TWENTY-ONE

Helena wasn't certain how it was possible to feel so happy and so terrified all at once. But it was. Inside she was a riot of emotion, such that she could scarcely breathe. She knew how badly this announcement to her family could go. There were a hundred terrible outcomes and so few positive ones, at least in this conversation.

But above all the fear, all the anticipation about how bad it could be, was something else. When she turned to look at Baldwin in this quiet moment they were sharing before Uncle Peter and Charity arrived in the parlor, her heart swelled with joy and happiness she'd never believed she'd experience again.

Baldwin loved her. That had felt like an impossibility since the first moment she met him and he made her heart skip a beat. She hadn't let herself hope for more than whatever stolen time they were allowed. Resigning herself to the fact that she couldn't have anything beyond that had been her only way to survive when her love for this man grew with each passing day.

And now…he was hers. He looked at her and she saw in his eyes that the fantasy, the fairytale, was true. And she knew that they could be happy together for the rest of their lives.

He slid his fingers through hers, lacing them together as he lifted her hand to kiss it. "I will *always* protect you, Helena."

It was a powerful statement, made even more so by the years she'd spent having only herself to depend upon. She nodded slowly. "I believe you, Your Grace."

He smiled as the door opened and her uncle and her cousin entered. All her good feelings fled, and she immediately went on alert. Out of habit, she shook away from Baldwin and took a step from his side. It was foolish, considering what he was about to declare, but judging from her uncle's angry expression as he saw them standing together, she feared the consequences that her newly minted fiancé didn't seem to fully grasp.

Uncle Peter was fully capable of mean and ugly pettiness. He would see her engagement as a betrayal, and if he could strike out at her…it was very likely he would do just that.

Baldwin frowned as she bent her head, but then he shifted his attention to the new additions to the room. "Mr. Shephard," he said, his tone icy cold. "And Miss Shephard. Welcome—I'm glad you were up and could join us for a moment before the rest of the party begins the merrymaking for the day."

"Have we interrupted something?" her uncle asked, spearing Helena with yet another glare. She felt it burning through her, accusatory.

"No," Baldwin answered for her. "Helena and I simply wished to share our happy news with you before we make our announcements to the party at large."

Helena held her breath as she watched for her family's reaction. Charity went pale, but her uncle lifted both eyebrows in question. He didn't look upset, although it was obvious what Baldwin was going to say.

"Announcement?" Charity repeated slowly.

"Yes," Baldwin said, and reached out to retake Helena's hand. He drew her closer, forcing her from the retreated position she had taken. Her breath shook and she almost screamed out at him not to say it. But the words fell from his mouth regardless. "I will marry Helena. As soon as possible."

For a moment the room was utterly silent. Then, without warning, her uncle tipped back his head and began to laugh. Helena flinched at the cruel sound of it and the twisted expression on his lips that could in no way be called a smile.

She knew then that he would find some way to make sure this never happened. He would do *everything* in his power and tear down anyone in his way.

Including Helena herself.

But Baldwin didn't know that. He didn't know Peter and his cruel, spoiled bent. While she shrank down a fraction, trying to make herself a smaller target, Baldwin straightened and his expression grew hard.

"And just what is so funny, Mr. Shephard?" he asked. "I do not appreciate your mockery."

"Oh, but there is so much to mock." Uncle Peter shook his head and said, "Do you think you can just...*have* her? No, no, Your Grace. I don't think so."

Baldwin released Helena's hand and took a long step toward her uncle. They stood chest-to-chest as Baldwin hissed, "I wasn't asking. You can support our union and your niece, or you and your daughter can leave."

Peter tilted his head, his expression empty and cold. He turned and walked around Baldwin to take a seat on the settee, where he folded his arms and looked up at the duke in defiance.

Helena's stomach turned. Whatever was about to happen, she knew it was not good. It would be ruinous, and her heart broke.

"You are missing some debts, I think, Your Grace," her uncle said softly.

Helena's ears began to ring and she jerked her gaze toward Baldwin. He was standing still, staring at Peter, his eyes wide with shock and his hands clenched at his sides. She could see he understood the same horrible thing she did in that moment.

"*I* own them," her uncle continued with a smug smile.

Baldwin didn't want to give this arrogant bastard the satisfaction of his reaction, but it was impossible not to have one.

The world was spinning, spinning out of control around him. There was no place to go to purchase, nothing that could make what Peter Shephard had said, or what he implied he would do, go away.

He fought for restraint and calm before he said, "I see."

"That brings you up short, doesn't it, Sheffield?" Shephard snorted out a laugh. "Not so superior anymore, are we?"

Baldwin had never been one to scrap. That was more James's style, or Robert's. But right now he wanted to smash a fist though this man's face more than he'd ever wanted anything in his life.

"Why?" Helena asked, her voice shaking as she moved to stand beside him. She didn't touch him, but he felt her presence nonetheless and it calmed him a little. "*Why* did you buy his debts?"

"Because I'm a businessman, my dear," her uncle said. "And business is all about leverage. Now I have it."

"I will pay you," Baldwin said softly, never happier that he had accepted Ewan's offer to repay the missing money in full if it were ever called back. That had felt like a humiliating sacrifice at the time, but now it didn't hold a candle to this current exchange. "I can have it to you as soon as we return to London."

"You don't have it," Shephard snorted. "Please. Don't think I haven't done my due diligence when it comes to your situation."

Baldwin clenched his fists at his side. "I have friends, damn you. You'll have your money."

Shephard shook his head. "No, no, *no*. I know all about your friends. They are far more successful than you are. Does that sting?"

"No." Baldwin clenched his teeth.

Shephard shrugged. "I don't know how it can't. But it doesn't really matter. *Their* money isn't what I want. *Your* money is what I want."

Helena covered her mouth. "Don't," she whispered through her fingers. "Oh, please don't do this."

Baldwin shot her a side glance and then looked at her uncle again. Shephard smiled as he pointed at her. "She knows me. She understands."

Baldwin folded his arms. "Then enlighten me, sir. Why would you give a damn where your money comes from? Especially given that you're such a businessman."

Shephard leaned back in his seat, utterly comfortable, like he owned the world and the room. "I want *you* to pay, Sheffield. Or else I will make certain that every man, woman and child in this country and abroad knows your true standing. And you know what that means, don't you?"

Baldwin swallowed. Oh yes, he did. It was the very worst-case scenario he had pictured. If his true financial situation was not revealed, he could continue on, frugally, carefully, but there was survival in that path. It was the only way he'd known he could offer for Helena and not destroy them both.

But if his other creditors realized his coffers were empty, there could be panic amongst them. Debts could be called back in full. Payments doubled out of fear that he would default. He and his family, including Helena if they were wed, wouldn't be welcomed in a shop in London. His mother would suffer the same fate potentially, despite her own inheritance being separate from the entail and the empty coffers. Even Charlotte would not be immune to the questions and whispers, despite her solid standing as Duchess of Donburrow.

It was his every nightmare brought to life.

"You understand," Shephard said. "I see you playing it all out in your mind. I can make it even worse depending on how I let it be known."

Baldwin swallowed past the bile that had gathered high in his throat and glared at Shephard. "Then why didn't you do it already? The debts were bought over a week ago. Before we even came here, though I only just found out about when the party began. Why play this game?"

"Because the game is what matters. There are many outcomes we still have to discuss. Your utter destruction is just one. There *is* another."

"What is that?" Baldwin asked, uncertain if he wanted to know. But the man held power over him. There was only one way to come through this and that was to understand his adversary.

"You could have this debt forgiven in its entirety without one farthing exchanging hands."

Baldwin wrinkled his brow in utter confusion. He certainly didn't believe Shephard was offering him this out of the kindness of his heart. "What? How?"

Shephard motioned toward Charity. "It's very simple, Your Grace. It's the option that has always been on the table. You marry my daughter."

CHAPTER TWENTY-TWO

Baldwin's stomach heaved as he stared first at Shephard, then at Helena, whose face was pale as she staggered beneath the weight of her uncle's cruel manipulation. That was the worst part in all this. Baldwin had promised to protect her. Now, no matter what he did, he couldn't.

"Marry Charity," he said, the words no more palatable coming from his own lips than they had been coming from Shephard's.

His gaze slipped to Charity, and he was surprised to see her expression as shocked as he felt. Certainly she was not crowing about this turn of events, though he wasn't certain he trusted that she wasn't a party in her father's twisted scheme.

"You bastard," Helena whispered, her voice trembling.

Shephard spun on her, one finger extended in accusation. "You watch yourself, girl. I've kindly offered to pay your passage back home, but I can rescind that and just have you put on the street. You wouldn't much like how a lady survives when she has no relatives to pity her. And if you interfere with me too much, I may just take back the extravagant offer I'm about to make your love and destroy him for the fun of it. You don't want to carry the guilt of that, do you?"

She flinched and turned toward him. "Baldwin," she whispered.

He recoiled at her expression and her tone. She was about

to tell him that this offer was one he should consider. "No!" he snapped. "I won't marry her, Helena."

"No?" Shephard chuckled, continuing to insert himself between them. "Well, I need a title. I want it. I want to throw it in the faces of all those who have questioned me over the years due to my allegiances during the first war. I want the doors it will open, doors others have found closed thanks to renewed tensions between our two countries. Yours is the best of the lot, the highest of the eligible gentlemen."

"The rank of it means nothing," Baldwin insisted. "Great God, you can see it means nothing."

"It means a great deal on paper. It means a great deal to tell those you contract with that your daughter is less than thirty deaths away from being queen."

Baldwin stared at him, shocked by the depths of this man's ambition. "Twenty-seven places from the throne might as well be twenty-seven hundred."

Shephard shrugged. "Either way, I will have it. And I've told you, it's a generous demand, really. You will have a great treasure in trade."

"Your daughter?" Baldwin said.

"No!" Shephard glanced at Charity and sniffed. "She's fine enough, though a disappointment, as a boy would have brought far more to my life."

Charity turned her head, and Baldwin almost felt sorry for her. It seemed Helena wasn't this man's only target.

"No, I'm not trying to make a romantic argument about how happy you could be with Charity," Shepard snorted. "I'm talking about the debts that will just go away. I'm talking about the fifty thousand pounds that will magically appear in your coffers. In my judgment, that will take a great deal of pressure off of you. And it will free you up to invest…or gamble, as I've heard you were once happy to do."

Baldwin tensed. The man had done his research very well, it seemed. And he was now stabbing him with it and taking pleasure in finding every soft spot.

"In short, I will save you," Shephard continued. "Or destroy you. It's your choice. So what's your pleasure?"

Helena could hardly breathe as she looked from her uncle's cold and horrible countenance and back to Baldwin's. She saw the pain there. The devastation as he realized that all he had planned for could not come to be. One way or another, there was no future as they'd hoped for. Either he would give up her, or give up everything else in his universe.

She couldn't let him make that sacrifice.

"Baldwin," she said, moving on him. When she caught his hand, he jumped, almost like he'd forgotten she was there. When he looked at her, the pain doubled. "You *must* consider what he's suggesting."

His face twisted in horror even more. "*No!*"

"I know," she said, touching his face and trying desperately not to cry at the idea that it might be the very last time she would do that. "I know. But you *must*. He is not bluffing. He'll ruin you and he'll never feel an ounce of remorse about it." She turned to her uncle. "Give us a moment."

Uncle Peter smirked and then shrugged. "Certainly. I can be generous in that. But time is ticking, Helena. Come along, Charity."

For a moment, her cousin just stood there, staring at Helena and Baldwin. Then she shook her head and followed her father from the room, leaving them alone again.

The moment they were, Baldwin turned to her. "I can see what you want to say to me. How you want to tell me I should sacrifice you. I will not do it, Helena. I can't do it."

She caught his hands. "My love, listen to me. We never intended for a future together. That was…" Her voice broke and she sucked in a breath. "That was a fantasy."

"It was reality," he insisted. "I asked you to be my wife.

You told me you would. We were ready to tell the world and move forward. And have you considered that when we made love today, we could have created a child? *Our* child."

Her hand stole to her belly as that concept slashed through her. Baldwin's baby, growing inside of her even now.

"If we had known what he held over you," she whispered, "we wouldn't have done any of those things."

He ran a hand over his face and let out an angry sound of frustration. As he did so, the door to the parlor opened and the room was suddenly filled as Charlotte and Ewan, the Duchess of Sheffield, Simon, Meg, James, Emma, Graham, Adelaide and Matthew all entered, filling the parlor almost to capacity. Helena turned away, wiping at the tears that were starting to fall.

"We were told that Shephard and his daughter left and thought we might have something to celebrate," the Duchess of Sheffield said as she moved farther into the room. "But from your faces, it seems that is not true."

Helena reached for Baldwin's hand. He held it so tightly. Like if he refused to let it go, he would not have to let her go. She knew better.

"Some of you know the truth," he said softly. "Others…well, I'll explain later. All you need know is that Peter Shephard holds certain debts of mine that I am unable to pay. He is demanding I marry Charity or he will ruin me."

The room was silent for a moment as looks of shock crossed the faces of all who were there. Then Ewan stepped forward and began to sign.

"I know what you're saying without Charlotte even having to translate," Baldwin said with a heavy sigh. "He refuses to accept any kind of payment from an outside source. The marriage is the only way he'll clear the debts and keep his knowledge of my situation a secret."

Helena swallowed hard. "I've told Baldwin that I believe he should accept the offer. I've told him that saving himself and his family should be his priority."

Emma stepped forward, her dark eyes filled with tears. "Oh,

Helena. Oh, I'm so sorry."

"I have not agreed," Baldwin snapped. "I love Helena. I asked her to marry me and she said yes."

"Before we knew," Helena whispered, turning back to him to continue the argument they'd been having before the others came into the room. "I love you," she said, not caring in that moment that those words were said before all their friends and family. "Don't throw away your future for me."

He caught her shoulders gently. "*You* are my future," he insisted. "If I'm destroyed, I'll still have you. So let him take what he wants."

"He isn't going to take anything."

Helena and Baldwin turned toward the door. Charity stood there, hands on her hips. The others parted, allowing her entrance, though Helena saw how they glared at her. The glares turned more heated when Peter Shephard slid into the room behind her.

"What are you on about, girl?" he asked. "You aren't going to make an idiot of yourself in front of all these powerful people, are you?"

Simon fisted his hands at his sides and started for the door. "You fucking—"

"No!" Graham barked, catching Simon's arms.

"Listen to your friend, Your Grace. You don't want to move on me when I can do so much damage, do you?" her uncle said with another of his satisfied sneers.

Simon relaxed back, eyes still narrowed. Meg slipped up beside him and took his arm. He looked down at her, and for a moment they just held stares. Then he let out his breath and shook his head.

"He doesn't deserve anyone's protection," Crestwood muttered.

"I said we needed a moment," Helena said, locking eyes with her cousin. "Can you not give us that when you plan to take everything else?"

"You don't need a moment," Charity said, and moved

toward Helena slowly. "You asked me yesterday why I hated you. I never hated you."

Helena lifted both brows. "That is hard to believe when you are doing this."

"*I'm* not," Charity insisted. "I will admit I have been jealous of you. Who could not be? You're so pretty. And everyone likes you right away. It's always been that way. When you fell, I thought—but I never hated you. I even convinced my father to bring you with us. I thought it might…help."

Helena watched her cousin's face closely. She'd known Charity all her life. Helena knew when she was lying. When she was manipulating. Right now it didn't seem like she was.

"Well, I suppose I'm happy you do not despise me," she said. "But that changes nothing. Your father is going to force Baldwin into a choice that he'll regret, no matter what it is."

Now Charity turned to her father. Uncle Peter had been watching them like a hawk and he glared at his daughter. "What are you looking at?"

"You're not going to force anyone into anything." Charity's voice was very calm, though her hands shook despite the strong front she was putting on. "I will not marry the Duke of Sheffield. I will not take part in your scheme."

He lunged forward, face purple. Helena had no idea if he meant to simply menace or actually harm. He got to do neither, for Graham stepped forward, caught Peter by the throat and backed him hard against the wall behind him. His face was hard as steel as he said, "Not a finger against that woman or I will rip you to shreds."

Peter glanced up at him. Up and up, and then he held up his hands. "I wouldn't touch my daughter."

"No. You won't." Graham backed away and reached for Adelaide. She took his hand, and together they glared at Peter along with the rest.

Charity was very pale, but she lifted her chin. "I will, however, marry the Earl of Grifford."

Her father tilted his head. "Grifford?"

She nodded. "He asked me two nights ago. I've been dangling him on a string ever since. But I will accept his offer. He's powerful enough for you, I think. And he adores me, so I know that I can make sure you have all the access you'll ever want. In exchange for my own demands."

Shephard folded his arms. "You have demands?"

She nodded. "You will forgive his debts." She pointed at Baldwin. "And you will gift Helena with a ten thousand pound dowry."

The entire room let out a collective gasp, but none more loud and forceful than Helena. She staggered, gripping Baldwin's arm as she stared at Charity.

Her cousin smiled at her. "See? I told you I didn't hate you."

Helena could find no words, but Charity didn't seem to need them. She glared at her father. "That is the only way you get anything you want."

"I'm not going to give that whore ten thousand pounds!" Peter roared.

"Shut your damned mouth!" Baldwin bellowed, and it was loud enough that Peter flinched. "Talk about her that way again and I will be the one to rip you to shreds and no one will stop me."

The other men in the room were nodding, and Peter shifted. "Talk about her or not, I'm still not giving her a farthing."

Charity let out a snort. "Please. Ten thousand is a mere drop in the vast bucket of your fortune. If you don't think I know your worth down to the last hay penny, you are sorely mistaken. You can afford the cost. And you will."

She smiled, and Helena recognized the expression well. It was the spoiled sneer that Charity always got when she knew she would get what she wanted. For the first time, Helena found herself rooting for her cousin.

"And if I don't?" Peter asked, but he sounded far less certain than he had a moment before.

Charity shrugged. "I suppose I could marry a handsome chimney sweep. Or run off to join the circus."

Adelaide let out a laugh. "I could probably help you arrange the second."

Graham cleared his throat. "Perhaps you should stay out of this, *Lydia*."

Helena didn't understand their joke, but she didn't care. She was too busy smiling. And when she glanced at Baldwin, she found him smiling, too. In fact everyone in the room was now smiling.

Save for her uncle, who glared at Charity. "You would do this to me. Your own father. When all I've tried to do is give you the best. You wouldn't dare!"

Charity laughed. "Test me. You raised me—do you really think I wouldn't *dare*?"

Peter's nostrils flared as he gaped at his daughter. But it was clear he had no response. "An earl," he grumbled.

"Yes." Charity smiled. "A powerful one at that. And just think, when Helena is married to a duke, you'll be linked to not one but two very powerful men. I'm certain Baldwin will not forget you."

Baldwin nodded slowly. "Certainly, I will not."

"It's your best option, Papa. So I'll ask you the same thing you asked the Duke of Sheffield a moment ago. What's your pleasure?"

Helena gaped as Peter's shoulders sagged. "Fine," he ground out. "Fine. I'll make the arrangements for everything."

He turned heel without another word and stormed out of the room, slamming the door behind him. The moment he was gone, the room let out its collective breath.

"Charity," Helena whispered as she crossed the room and embraced her cousin as hard as she could. "Thank you so much. You have saved us."

Charity pulled away and smoothed her dress. Discomfort with the display of affection was clear on her. "Oh, please."

"No," Helena insisted. "You are making a sacrifice for me and I shall not forget it ever."

Charity shrugged. "A sacrifice to be a countess? No. Truth

be told, I rather like the Earl of Grifford. He's dashing. And I'll outlive him and become a scandalous widow, no doubt."

"Well, you are certainly welcome in our circles," Emma said as she came forward. She caught Charity's hands. "You were so very brave."

Charity was blushing like a beet now. She fluttered her hands. "Oh, you're too much. I must follow my father now. Smooth his very ruffled feathers, and leave you to your celebrating." She smiled at Helena. "You caught a duke, Helena. Good show."

Charity flounced from the room. When she was gone, there was an eruption of laughter as the group moved forward to hug Helena and slap Baldwin's back. She watched him as they did so, watched how quiet he was even as he smiled through the congratulations.

"We should have champagne with lunch!" Charlotte gasped. "An engagement announcement should always have champagne associated with it. Mama and I will arrange it all."

Baldwin nodded. "Of course. There is a great deal to celebrate."

Charlotte was practically bouncing as she started for the door. "Come, everyone! I will need everyone's help with the planning, and it will give Helena and Baldwin a moment."

The others left, too, with the exception of the Duchess of Sheffield. She turned to the couple with a smile. "I wanted to say something to you both."

Helena tensed, for she knew Baldwin's mother had worked for a very different outcome for her son. She had no idea if the duchess really accepted her.

"What is it, Mama?" Baldwin asked softly.

"I have only ever wanted the happiness of my children," she said as she squeezed Baldwin's hand gently. "It kept me up at night to think that you would not have love like your sister has found. This resolution came with a great deal of trouble and worry, but I'm so happy for you both." She moved to Helena and reached out to touch her cheek. "Welcome to our family, you dear, sweet girl."

Helena let out her breath in relief as the duchess hugged her briefly. She was brushing away tears when she released Helena with a laugh. "And now I must go make sure you sister doesn't plan your entire wedding without any input from you."

She gave a little wave as she left the room and firmly shut the door behind herself. When she was gone, Helena took a deep breath and faced Baldwin again.

"All right, out with it. What is wrong? I can see you are troubled. So tell me. Have you changed your mind already?"

Baldwin stared at Helena. She asked him the question in a light, teasing tone, but he could see the genuine concern slashed across her face.

He caught her hands and drew her close. "Look at me, Helena. I love you and I cannot wait to marry you. Nothing has changed that."

She sagged in relief for a moment before she tilted her head. "Then what is it that keeps you from being fully happy?"

He pressed his lips together. "I vowed to protect you. But I didn't. Your cousin did, against all odds."

Helena seemed to consider that for a moment. "To my utter surprise, Charity *did* sweep in and take on the role as savior. But I think no less of you. You stood toe-to-toe with my uncle and declared that you would allow him to destroy your world so that you could marry me. Do you truly think I don't realize you meant it? That you really would have sacrificed everything for me?"

He shrugged one shoulder. "I would have gladly given anything for you, Helena."

"But you didn't have to," she said. "And for that, I'm very grateful. Charity may have helped make that easier, but *you* saved me."

He shook his head as he looked down at her, this woman he had come to love so deeply and so powerfully. "No, my love. You saved me. From the moment I found you counting stars, you saved me."

She lifted up on her tiptoes and brushed her lips to his. "We will compromise and say we saved each other," she said softly. "And we will promise to do the same every day, every night, for the rest of our lives."

"The rest of our lives," he agreed, then claimed her lips once more.

CHAPTER TWENTY-THREE

Six Weeks Later

"They actually make a rather happy-looking couple," James said as he handed over a glass of wine to Helena and then moved to stand beside Baldwin. Together, the three of them watched as Charity took her first turn around the dancefloor with her new husband, the Earl of Grifford.

Helena raised her glass in silent tribute to her cousin. "She'll probably run the poor man into the ground before five years are up. But yes, she does seem to like him."

"Then it is a happy ending for all," Baldwin sighed. "Though I argue you and I made a much happier couple on our wedding day."

Helena glanced up at him, remembering that beautiful day just two weeks before. "Indeed. The happiest."

James turned toward them with a smile. "And we are all overjoyed for you. Our little group of dukes has had an interesting year, hasn't it? Five marriages in just over twelve months."

"We will all be tamed yet," Baldwin chuckled.

"I actually wanted to talk to you about something," James said.

His gaze shifted to Helena, and she glanced at Baldwin. "Should I go?"

"No," he said. "I'm certain James can share his business with both of us. No more secrets. I've learned the hard way how they can destroy."

She squeezed his hand gently. She knew how hard it had been for Baldwin since all that happened in Sheffield over a month before. When he'd told his entire group of friends about his lack of fortune, about his own actions that had contributed to it, she'd felt his palpable humiliation and heartbreak.

Of course they had been accepting and tried to help. She'd been proud of how gently and kindly Baldwin had turned them down. The ten thousand her uncle had reluctantly allowed her to take into the marriage had helped a great deal, but she knew their life would not be easy.

"Do you see the gentleman standing over there? With the pretty dark-haired lady in blue?" James asked.

Helena and Baldwin followed his gaze, and she nodded. "I recognize the lady. Rosalinde Danford. I met her at one of Charlotte's teas. She and her sister are lovely."

"Her husband is Grayson Danford," James said. "He's brother to the Earl of Stenfax."

"I think I've crossed paths with him a few times," Baldwin said as he examined the man from afar. "Seems a decent sort."

"He is, I think," James said, looking off at the man. "He's also a shrewd businessman. I ran into him at White's last week and we began talking about canals. And steam. And a lot of other things the man is involved in."

"You're going to invest?" Baldwin asked.

James speared him with a glance. "Yes. And so are you. Five thousand pounds."

Helena felt Baldwin stiffen at her side, and she clung harder to his arm so he would feel her strength if his own wavered. "I think I've already had a conversation with you about taking your charity. I appreciate everyone's desire to save me, but if I'm ever to be able to look myself in the mirror again, I need to save myself."

James nodded. "I know. That's why this isn't a gift. It's a

loan. I'll even charge you interest. But I'm telling you that the opportunities Danford is talking about here...they could pay back tenfold. Twenty-fold."

Helena glanced up at Baldwin. "Twenty-fold? That would be a hundred thousand. Enough to..."

"Yes," Baldwin breathed, shock lacing his tone.

She could see he was still uncertain. Apparently so could James. He clapped a hand on Baldwin's shoulder. "Life is not a straight line, my friend. And it isn't always fair. I think we all know that very well. We can rebuild, though, if we aren't too stubborn not to take the opportunity."

Baldwin looked down at Helena and she smiled back at him. He nodded slowly. "Very well. I would appreciate the opportunity to rebuild."

James's expression softened. "Excellent. Come by the house tomorrow and I'll have my man draw up paperwork. We can call on Danford together and you'll see what I mean. But for now, I'm off to dance with my wife before she expires from waiting. Helena."

She smiled. "James."

When he was gone, she turned to Baldwin, searching for a hint of humiliation or anger or upset. She found none. Just a real excitement in his eyes.

"You don't mind, do you? That I agreed to take on yet another debt?"

"It sounds like an exciting venture," she said. "I think it was a good bargain to make."

He let out a long breath of relief and then his gaze became focused only on her. "Whatever happens, I want you to know...the real rebuilding of my life began and will end with you."

She smiled at him, overjoyed with the present, excited for the future. And when he bent to kiss her, she lost herself in the moment and in him. Because he was where she belonged.

Enjoy an exciting excerpt from

The Undercover Duke,

out March 2018

Lucas shifted as the carriage turned and he was rocked against the wall. Every muscle in his body protested with screaming pain and he gripped his fists against the leather carriage seat to keep from crying out.

How he hated being injured. Being weak. How he hated that it all felt so commonplace to him now. Pain was just part of life.

The carriage came to a stop and he looked out the window as the servants began to move to help him. It was a small cottage that they'd come to. One that looked like every other cottage in Garygreen, a part of London he'd never been to before. He knew all the worst parts through his job, and the best thanks to his upbringing.

He hated them both equally. But this place was suspended somewhere in between. Not too high and mighty, but neat and tidy, well maintained. Anonymous.

The door opened and the men Stalwood had tasked with helping him appeared. Their faces were grim as one said, "Ready, Your Grace?"

Lucas winced at both the recognition of the pain about to come and the title that was used to address him. "Yes," he ground out, his voice rough as he reached out to steady himself on waiting arms. He staggered forward, trying in vain to keep his grunts of agony in as he was helped down.

The men looked away as they guided him up the stairs to the cottage door. They were spies, like he was, sent to do this menial task because they were the only ones to be trusted with the secret of his location. He knew what they saw when they looked at him: their future. And it wasn't one they wanted, so they distanced themselves.

The door to the cottage was already open and the men

helped him in. They didn't hesitate as they all but carried him up another short flight of stairs and down a hall to an open door. Lucas had to believe this had all been prearranged. He did not yet even know who it was who would be taking care of him during his time here. Stalwood had said a healer, but nothing more.

A healer. He all but scoffed. He'd been poked and prodded and tortured by many a man who called himself that. The amount of healing that had followed was laughable. He was broken, perhaps irretrievably, and that sent a wash of rage and pain through him more powerful than any caused by the physical.

"Let me go," he snapped, staggering from the arms of those helping him and all but collapsing against the edge of the bed.

The men seemed unmoved by his ill humor. All but one left him there. The last was named Simmons. Lucas glared at him. He'd trained this particular pup years ago, and now the boy stared at him like he was a dotard, lost to his youth and usefulness.

"Is there anything I can do?" Simmons asked, all that pity heavy in his mournful tone.

"No," Lucas said through clenched teeth as he turned his face. "Just get out."

"Well, that is a pretty way to talk to someone who is helping you!"

Lucas turned at the sharp, feminine voice that had said those harsh words. There, standing in the doorway, staring at him like he was a monster, was a woman. Not just a woman, a goddess, it would seem. She had dark hair with deep red highlights, a finely shaped face and full lips. Her eyes were the most spectacular green he had ever seen. Like jade stolen from faraway lands that he could only dream of now.

At this moment, those green eyes were narrowed and filled with anger as she folded her arms and shook her head. Her censure made him feel a strange sense of…shame. An odd sensation he rarely experienced. He'd cut that away a long time ago.

"Mr. Simmons, is it not?" she asked, turning to the other

man in the room.

"Yes, miss," Simmons said, and his gaze flitted over their companion. Lucas recognized the interest that lit in his eyes. The same he felt in his own belly.

Only the younger man likely had a better chance than he did in his current state.

"Thank you for your help. I believe I can handle the situation from here. Please send word to Lord Stalwood that we are settled."

Simmons glanced at Lucas and then back to the woman. "Of course, miss. I will be one of the guards rotating here. If you have any trouble, if you *need* anything, put a candle in the front window and I will come at once."

The young woman nodded, and seemed oblivious to Simmons' regard as she motioned him toward the hallway. "I appreciate that kindness. Good day."

Simmons shrugged ever so slightly and left. Once he was gone, the young woman turned toward Lucas, those sharp eyes still filled with slight disgust and judgment.

"Hello," she said, stepping into the room. "I trust the room will be comfortable, even if it does not meet your standards."

Lucas leaned on the bed with his undamaged arm, mostly because he was not entirely certain he could stay upright on his own. "I have no standards, I'm afraid. Ask anyone in my acquaintance."

Her lips pursed in what seemed like annoyance at his quip and she moved toward him. "Let me help you."

He recoiled as she reached out. "I can get myself into the bed."

Her brow wrinkled, and when her gaze swept over him, he felt her judgment even more powerfully. She glanced at his face and shrugged. "So you say. Then I shall let you get settled on your own if that is your choice at present. I will return in an hour to bring you some food and to check your wounds."

She said nothing else, nor did she wait for his answer to her statement. She merely turned on her heel and marched from the room, tugging the door behind herself as she left.

When she was gone, Lucas collapsed against the mattress, too exhausted and pained to even try to remove his boots. He had no idea who the lady was, nor her role in the next few weeks of his life. Perhaps she was the healer's wife or daughter. Perhaps she was a servant. He supposed he would find out soon enough.

Whatever the answer, her presence, as lovely as it was, did not change the facts of his life. He did not want to be here, and he was going to do everything in his power to get away from this place as soon as possible.

Other Books by Jess Michaels

THE 1797 CLUB

For information about the upcoming series, go to
www.1797club.com to join the club!

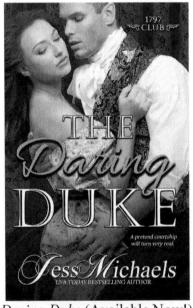

The Daring Duke (Available Now!)
Her Favorite Duke (Available Now!)
The Broken Duke (Available Now!)
The Silent Duke (Available Now!)
The Duke of Nothing (Coming January 2018)
The Undercover Duke (Coming March 2018)
The Duke of Hearts (Coming May 2018)
The Duke Who Lied (Coming August 2018)
The Duke of Desire (Coming October 2018)
The Last Duke (Coming November 2018)

SEASONS

An Affair in Winter (Book 1)
A Spring Deception (Book 2)
One Summer of Surrender (Book 3)
Adored in Autumn (Book 4)

THE WICKED WOODLEYS

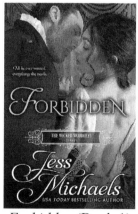

Forbidden (Book 1)
Deceived (Book 2)
Tempted (Book 3)
Ruined (Book 4)
Seduced (Book 5)

THE NOTORIOUS FLYNNS
The Other Duke (Book 1)
The Scoundrel's Lover (Book 2)
The Widow Wager (Book 3)
No Gentleman for Georgina (Book 4)
A Marquis for Mary (Book 5)

THE LADIES BOOK OF PLEASURES
A Matter of Sin
A Moment of Passion
A Measure of Deceit

THE PLEASURE WARS SERIES
Taken By the Duke
Pleasuring The Lady
Beauty and the Earl
Beautiful Distraction

About the Author

USA Today Bestselling author Jess Michaels likes geeky stuff, Vanilla Coke Zero, anything coconut, cheese, fluffy cats, smooth cats, any cats, many dogs and people who care about the welfare of their fellow humans. She watches too much daytime court shows, but just enough Dirk Gently. She is lucky enough to be married to her favorite person in the world and live in a beautiful home on a golf course lake in Northern Arizona.

When she's not obsessively checking her steps on Fitbit or trying out new flavors of Greek yogurt, she writes erotic historical romances with smoking hot alpha males and sassy ladies who do anything but wait to get what they want. She has written for numerous publishers and is now fully indie and loving every moment of it (well, almost every moment).

Jess loves to hear from fans! So please feel free to contact her in any of the following ways (or carrier pigeon):

www.AuthorJessMichaels.com

Email: Jess@AuthorJessMichaels.com
Twitter www.twitter.com/JessMichaelsbks
Facebook: www.facebook.com/JessMichaelsBks

Jess Michaels raffles a gift certificate EVERY month to members of her newsletter, so sign up on her website: http://www.authorjessmichaels.com/

Made in the USA
Middletown, DE
20 April 2018